Big Daddy Brubaker is still up to his matchmaking tricks. Will Charlotte Beauchamp stand a chance against the feisty patron's plan to turn her into his nephew's bride?

♥ ♥ ♥ ♥ ♥

Miss Clarise and Big Daddy watched through the parlor window as Charlotte sulked after Tex. They headed away from the mansion to the stables beyond.

"She's a spunky little thing," Big Daddy murmured from where he stood behind his wife. "Think our Tex can handle her?"

"She's a Beauchamp."

"Yeahup. Kinda reminds me of another purty little gal I know."

Miss Clarise turned in her husband's arms. "Oh, Big Daddy. You're still such a tease." With a gentle inclination of her head, she rested her nose against his. "Was it my imagination, or were there some sparks flying between those two?"

"Well, he's a Brubaker and she's a Beauchamp. I'd say they don't stand much of a chance."

"Mmm. I'm thinking an outdoor wedding."

"She does have that pet pig. What about a luau theme?"

"I'll begin making notes."

Dear Reader,

Although the anniversary is over, Silhouette Romance is still celebrating our coming of age—we'll soon be twenty-one! Be sure to join us each and every month for six emotional stories about the romantic journey from first time to forever.

And this month we've got a special Valentine's treat for you! Three stories deal with the special holiday for true lovers. Karen Rose Smith gives us a man who asks an old friend to *Be My Bride?* Teresa Southwick's latest title, *Secret Ingredient: Love,* brings back the delightful Marchetti family. And Carla Cassidy's *Just One Kiss* shows how a confirmed bachelor is brought to his knees by a special woman.

Amusing, emotional and oh-so-captivating Carolyn Zane is at it again! Her latest BRUBAKER BRIDES story, *Tex's Exasperating Heiress,* features a determined groom, a captivating heiress and the pig that brought them together. And popular author Arlene James tells of *The Mesmerizing Mr. Carlyle,* part of our AN OLDER MAN thematic miniseries. Readers will love the overwhelming attraction between this couple! Finally, *The Runaway Princess* marks Patricia Forsythe's debut in the Romance line. But Patricia is no stranger to love stories, having written many as Patricia Knoll!

Next month, look for appealing stories by Raye Morgan, Susan Meier, Valerie Parv and other exciting authors. And be sure to return in March for a new installment of the popular ROYALLY WED tales!

Happy reading!

Mary-Theresa Hussey

Mary-Theresa Hussey
Senior Editor

Please address questions and book requests to:
Silhouette Reader Service
U.S.: 3010 Walden Ave., P.O. Box 1325, Buffalo, NY 14269
Canadian: P.O. Box 609, Fort Erie, Ont. L2A 5X3

Tex's
Exasperating Heiress

CAROLYN ZANE

SILHOUETTE *Romance*®

Published by Silhouette Books

America's Publisher of Contemporary Romance

For my faithful companion and partner in writing and
power walking, my golden retriever, Bob Barker.
(Not to be confused with the game show host.)
I love ya, man!

Lord, thou knowest all things;
thou knowest that I love thee.
—*John* 21:17

SILHOUETTE BOOKS

ISBN 0-373-19494-3

TEX'S EXASPERATING HEIRESS

Copyright © 2001 by Carolyn Suzanne Pizzuti

All rights reserved. Except for use in any review, the reproduction
or utilization of this work in whole or in part in any form by any
electronic, mechanical or other means, now known or hereafter
invented, including xerography, photocopying and recording, or in
any information storage or retrieval system, is forbidden without
the written permission of the editorial office, Silhouette Books,
300 East 42nd Street, New York, NY 10017 U.S.A.

All characters in this book have no existence outside the imagination of
the author and have no relation whatsoever to anyone bearing the same
name or names. They are not even distantly inspired by any individual
known or unknown to the author, and all incidents are pure invention.

This edition published by arrangement with Harlequin Books S.A.

® and TM are trademarks of Harlequin Books S.A., used under license.
Trademarks indicated with ® are registered in the United States Patent
and Trademark Office, the Canadian Trade Marks Office and in other
countries.

Visit Silhouette at www.eHarlequin.com

Printed in U.S.A.

Books by Carolyn Zane

*Sister Switch
†The Brubaker Brides

CAROLYN ZANE

lives with her husband, Matt, their preschool daughter, Madeline, and their latest addition, baby daughter Olivia, in the rolling countryside near Portland, Oregon's Willamette River. Like Chevy Chase's character in the movie *Funny Farm,* Carolyn finally decided to trade in a decade of city dwelling and producing local television commercials for the quaint country life of a novelist. And even though they have bitten off decidedly more than they can chew in the remodeling of their hundred-year-plus-old farmhouse, life is somewhat saner for her than for poor Chevy. The neighbors are friendly, the mail carrier actually stops at the box and the dog, Bob Barker, sticks close to home.

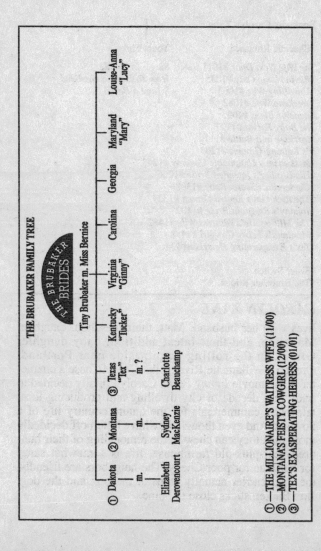

THE BRUBAKER FAMILY TREE

THE BRUBAKER BRIDES

Tiny Brubaker m. Miss Bernice

① Dakota — m. — Elizabeth Derwencourt

② Montana — m. — Sydney MacKenzie

③ Texas "Tex" — m. ? — Charlotte Beauchamp

Kentucky "Tucker"

Virginia "Ginny"

Carolina

Georgia

Maryland "Mary"

Louise-Anna "Lucy"

① —THE MILLIONAIRE'S WAITRESS WIFE (11/00)
② —MONTANA'S FEISTY COWGIRL (12/00)
③ —TEX'S EXASPERATING HEIRESS (01/01)

Chapter One

Charlotte Beauchamp was stuck with a pig.

Not as the word might pertain to a chauvinistic man. Nor as some might use the word to describe a broken-down car, an overly enthusiastic law officer or a ravenous, somewhat slovenly dinner companion.

No, Charlotte Beauchamp was stuck with a *real* pig.

The farm animal variety, turned indoor pet. A potbellied number that snorted, rolled in mud whenever it got the chance and ate a nauseating mixture of leftovers—commonly referred to as "slop"—for breakfast.

"Pardon me?" Miss Clarise Brubaker, Charlotte's second cousin—once removed—was obviously taken back. "When Aunt Dorothy died, she did what?"

Charlotte sighed. "She left me a pig."

Miss Clarise and Big Daddy, her husband of over forty years, exchanged incredulous glances.

"A...pig."

"Yes, ma'am."

"Just a pig?"

"For now, yes."

The three were seated in the parlor of the Brubakers' opulent mansion upon comfortable, overstuffed furniture. Afternoon sunshine streamed through the floor-to-ceiling windows, casting an ethereal glow about the room and setting the crystal objets d'art on fire and causing the silver and gold accent pieces to sparkle. Lovely marble statues were positioned between the windows. Long, gauzy white curtains puddled richly on the mahogany floor and billowed in the slight Texas breezes that wafted across the endless acreage of the Circle BO ranch.

Though they were only distant relatives, the well-known oil baron and his wife always made Charlotte feel as though she were part of the gargantuan Brubaker family that included nine offspring, their spouses and children, and a host of nieces and nephews. There was something so infinitely lovable about the millionaire munchkin, Big Daddy, and his sweet wife, Miss Clarise.

At the moment, the lovable pair leaned forward in their seats and stared agog at Charlotte.

"My aunt Dorothy left you a pig?" With a clatter, Miss Clarise set her teacup on the silver tray in front of her, and struggled to keep her soft-spoken drawl...soft. "But, sweetheart, as her great-granddaughter, and—considering your lovely parents have passed on to glory— *you* were her only living heir! And, darlin', your nanna Dorothy was rich!"

"Filthy rich," Big Daddy put in.

"I can't believe she could be so cruel. Especially considering that you gave up your personal life to nurse her for the last ten of her one hundred years. Surely, you can contest this will. Quite clearly, she wasn't in her right mind when she left you a...a...*pig!*"

"Well, actually, Miss Clarise, in a roundabout way,

she did leave everything to me. You see, within the will, there is a proviso that states I must 'adopt,' for lack of a better word, Toto and raise him as if he were my own child.''

"Toto?"

"The pig."

"I…see." Miss Clarise simply stared.

"Yes. Very soon Nanna Dorothy's estate will be sold and the proceeds put into a trust account with the rest of her assets. I'll inherit everything, if—and only if—I promise to love, honor and obey the—'' she wrinkled her nose at the thought of the despicable animal ''—uh… Toto for the rest of his life. When he passes away of natural causes, the considerable trust will be turned over to me.''

Miss Clarise absently fingered the diamond broach at her throat. "My land. Heaven forbid an accident should befall Toto.''

"True. Toto is worth his considerable weight in gold, as long as he dies naturally.'' Charlotte bunched her shoulders in a pragmatic fashion. "Unfortunately, he's still relatively young in pig years, so it's going to be a while. The bottom line is, I need to start looking for a job.''

"What will you do?''

Charlotte hoped her cheerful countenance belied some of her trepidation. "I'm not sure. I went straight from boarding school to live with and care for Nanna. I'm not really qualified to do much of anything except care for the elderly, and frankly, after ten years of that, I'm ready for a change. To what…I'm not sure.''

Charlotte raked her thick curly hair out of her eyes and tossed it over her shoulder. "But, I'm not worried,'' she chirped, trying to sound the independent millennium woman. "I'll land on my feet. We Beauchamps always do."

She cast a thousand-watt smile upon Miss Clarise, who had been a Beauchamp before she married Big Daddy.

"To be perfectly honest, I'm not worried about inheriting the money. If it happens, fine. If not, I'll make do somehow. I just hope I can live through the next few years without honey-glazing Toto and serving him for Christmas dinner."

"I don't think that's what Dorothy had in mind when she asked you to take care of him." Miss Clarise smoothed her smart, tailored skirt over her still shapely knees. "Why do you suppose Aunt Dorothy would do such an unusual thing with her will?" she mused aloud.

Charlotte gave her head a puzzled shake. "Hard to say. She adored Toto. Treated him like her child. The way some people treat their dogs. On the one hand, she knew I was a good caregiver, but, on the other hand, she also knew that I am *not* an animal person. Which brings me to one of the reasons I'm here, aside from visiting the two of you."

Turning in her seat, Charlotte faced Big Daddy. "Toto's vet mentioned your nephew, Tex."

"Yes, we have a nephew named Tex. Lives here on the Circle BO. He's one of my brother Tiny's boys."

"Great. The vet said Tex has an excellent reputation as an animal trainer. Especially farm animals. They say he can turn even the most savage beast into a docile little lamb."

Big Daddy nodded. "That's our Tex. Ever since he was knee-high to a toadstool, that kid could break horses. He's also great with cow dogs. He's got a growing practice that he's building right here on the ranch, out beyond the stable a piece. Went to school, came out with a fistful of degrees and now he does a lot of research for the university in his clinic.''

Charlotte couldn't help but smile. Big Daddy was so obviously proud of his nephew.

''It's a pretty big deal,'' the older man continued. ''Tex's what they call an animal behaviorist.''

''Oh? Hmm. I think I might need more of an animal exorcist.'' Charlotte exhaled and dropped her head back against the lush sofa cushion. ''I'm reasonably certain that Toto is possessed.'' She rubbed her temples and moaned. ''I think Nanna Dorothy thought this whole thing was uproariously amusing.''

Big Daddy pinched his wide, pliant lips between his thumb and forefinger for a moment, as if to pull the smile off his face.

Miss Clarise quelled her husband's mirth with a narrow glance. ''Charlotte darlin', forgive me for worryin', but what are you supposed to do for the next few years, with no house and no income and no real job experience, other than nursing a family member full-time?''

''Oh, Miss Clarise, I'll be all right. To be honest, I'm eager to land my first real job. Make some friends. Taking care of Nanna Dorothy precluded much of a social life, I'm afraid.'' Her smile was rueful. ''Tomorrow I'm going apartment hunting. Hopefully I can find an affordable place that takes pigs.''

Unable to stop himself, Big Daddy guffawed with glee.

''Hush, Big Daddy.'' Miss Clarise whapped her husband, then reached out and grasped her second-cousin-once-removed's hands in her own. ''Charlotte, darlin', you must move in here with us. Why, since so many of our own children have married and moved out on their own, we'd be thrilled to have the company. You have your choice of at least five empty suites.'' She twisted in her seat to face her husband. ''Isn't that right, sugar?''

''That's right, dumplin'.''

Charlotte felt her eyes well with unexpected tears. These two were always so sweet and generous. She blinked and drew a deep breath. ''Oh, thank you so much for your lovely offer, but I really couldn't.''

Big Daddy snorted. ''Course ya can. I won't heah of one of my darlin' wife's relatives—let alone one as beautiful and young as yourself—rattlin' around alone in that big ol' house until it sells. It ain't safe. Leastwise, not while you got a passel of prospective buyers traipsing through at all hours. You'll move in to the big house until you have time to sort your future out, lamb chop. No argument.''

The poignant lump in Charlotte's throat made it hard to swallow. Miss Clarise and Big Daddy were all the family she had left in the world. Their kind concern was overwhelming. Nanna Dorothy had loved her in her way, Charlotte knew, but never with the sweet affection that the Brubakers shared so easily.

''Okay,'' she managed softly, and took a deep breath. ''But only until I get my feet on the ground. Then, I want…no, I *need* to strike out on my own. I have to prove I can take care of myself.''

''I understand that.'' Big Daddy winked and a click of approval sounded from between his teeth.

''By the way—'' Charlotte darted a sheepish glance at her benefactors ''—you do realize that Toto's part of the package?''

''Of course,'' Miss Clarise assured her. ''No problem at all. We have plenty of space. And surely, Tex will be happy to take Toto on as a client.''

Perhaps Miss Clarise spoke too soon, Charlotte mused.

Or perhaps the fates were against her. Perhaps the disgusting, madcap Toto was Satan's spawn whose sole destiny was to make her life a living hell. Because, as the three of them sipped aromatic tea from fine china cups, and nibbled on delicate cookies, the ugly, salivating, whirling dervish that was Toto came barreling into the parlor.

Hot on the renegade Toto's hooves, a glowering cowboy thundered into the parlor and skidded to a stop just shy of the sofa. He gave a deferential nod in Charlotte's direction before he spoke.

"Miss Clarise, Big Daddy, I'm sorry to interrupt your little visit, but I found this poor pig locked in a car outside. Some moron left him to die."

Charlotte frowned as she jumped to her feet. *Moron?* Insulted, she shot the buttinski ranch hand a withering glance, before she darted off after the lawless Toto, who was now running amuck at the other end of the expansive parlor.

"Oh, Miss Clarise, I'm…so terribly sorry…that my pig got…out…" Charlotte huffed and lunged for the bristly missile, as he headed back to where they'd all been sitting. His curly tail slipped through her fingertips as he dove under the table that held the delicate tea service. "I'll…pay…for any…damage…that he—" again, Toto dodged her grasp "—that he…might do."

"*Your* pig?" The ranch hand thumbed his Stetson back and smirked.

"Yes." Charlotte grunted and yanked Toto from under the table by his collar, but not before he upset a cup of tea and sent its contents raining onto the Turkish rug.

Toto squealed like the tires on a souped-up sports car.

Breathless, Charlotte shot a weak smile of apology at Miss Clarise and Big Daddy. "I'll…just…take…" she panted, laboring against the lunging pig, "him...back... out...to my...carrrr."

"*What?*" The arrogant cowboy with the incredible dimples planted his hands on his narrow hips and stared at her as if she were some sort of felon. "It's nearly a hundred degrees out there. If you're serious—" his upper lip curled "—I'll get a skewer and we'll set up a spit. By this evening we should be ready for the luau."

His sarcastic tone had Charlotte suddenly defensive. Incensed, she fumbled in her pocket for the pig's leash, then bolted after the escaping Toto in an attempt to clip it to his rhinestone collar.

Luau. Very funny. This ranch hand had no business talking to her this way. She was not a child! She was perfectly capable of taking care of this odious oinker. Between this man's arrogant, condescending attitude and Toto—who was currently getting ready to take a "break" on the linen puddled between the windows—her blood pressure was rising like the mercury outside.

"*No!*" She jerked Toto away from the window. "Bad, bad, *bad* pig!"

Charlotte could feel the cowboy rolling his eyes behind her back and longed to punch him in his perfectly chiseled, up-in-the-air nose. But, before she could entertain this fantasy to its satisfying conclusion, Toto yanked her over to a giant potted palm, where he began to root in the soil, flinging great clods to the spotless floor with his snout. Thoroughly humiliated, she wished for a tornado to whisk her—and Toto too—to the land of Oz.

"No, no, Toto!" she cried. Dropping to her knees, she scooped the dirt back into the container as fast as he shoved it out. "I'm so very sorry. Usually he doesn't act quite this badly."

"Probably because you keep him locked in a car."

Charlotte, hauled herself to her feet and stood swaying. With murder in her eye, she dragged her hair out of her face and stared at this boar. Obviously, it took one to know one. Her words fired in a semiautomatic fashion. "The door was *un*locked."

He snorted his disgust. "Oh, now that's helpful. For a *cloven hoofed beast!*"

"I parked in the shade!"

"The shade moved," the cowboy bit out, his eyes steely.

Tightly civilized, only because Miss Clarise and Big Daddy were watching with obvious interest, Charlotte struggled to remain the refined lady.

"I left the windows cracked and he has plenty of water."

"Had." The cowboy hooked his thumbs through his belt loops and took a rangy step toward her. "He spilled his water."

"That figures," Charlotte hissed. Using every muscle at her disposal, she dragged Toto away from the pot and fastened the other end of his leash to one of the heavy brass andirons that adorned the fireplace, then turned to face the ranch hand. "But even so, that shouldn't matter. I left the engine in my car running and the air-conditioning on."

"You ran out of gas."

The sounds of an andiron being dragged over mahogany drew Charlotte's attention. *"No!"* Horrified, she noted the new plow marks in the gleaming woodwork.

The luau idea grew more appealing by the minute.

After a brief wrestling match that had the other adults looking on in wonder, Charlotte managed to untie the porcine devil. Once free, he scampered about the room, dragging Charlotte with him as he went, crazily head-butting this and that, overturning the smaller antiques, sniffing, chewing and continuing the quest for the perfect spot upon which to do his business.

"Toto, no!" Charlotte looked helplessly at Miss Clarise as Toto crashed into a china cabinet, loaded with priceless bric-a-brac. "He's housebroken, really. I don't know why he's acting this way."

The cowboy smirked. "It's clear why he's acting this way."

At the boiling point, Charlotte stopped and stared. "Who *are* you?"

Miss Clarise jumped to her feet, her soft southern drawl giving this whole ridiculous situation an element of class. "Charlotte, dear, allow me to introduce you to my nephew on Big Daddy's side, Tex Brubaker. Tex, this is Charlotte Beauchamp, my second-cousin-once-removed, which would make you two...well, not related in the least, I guess. Hmm. That's too bad."

"Not really." Tex looked idly at Charlotte.

"*You're* Tex Brubaker?" Charlotte sighed and let her shoulders fall.

Miss Clarise and Big Daddy exchanged glances.

"Miss Clarise, I'm so sorry about all of this..." Charlotte gestured to the pig who pranced and lurched at the end of his leash, tugging her arm half out of its socket. "Big Daddy, please, forgive me."

"Nuthin' to forgive, little darlin'. Tex, take this hambone out to your kennel and give him a cool drink and a place to do his bidness." Big Daddy grabbed Toto by the scruff of the neck and muscled him over to his lanky nephew. "We'll send Charlotte along to pick him up when we're finished with our visit."

Tex allowed his lazy gaze to rove over Charlotte. Then

he took the leash and with one quiet word, had Toto seated docilely at his feet.

She bristled. Beginner's luck. Toto was tired now. But just wait until he got his second wind. Then they'd see how calm and unflappable this...this *Animal Behaviorist* was.

"And, Tex, darlin'—" Miss Clarise took several steps and laid a slender hand on her nephew's considerable bicep "—Charlotte will be staying with us for a while, until she can find steady employment and a little place of her own in Hidden Valley. I would deem it a personal favor, if you would take Charlotte and her...her...Toto on as your clients. In memory of my late aunt Dorothy, who loved her pet as if he were her child and then left his well-being in her will, to our Charlotte, here."

Tex looked down into his aunt's twinkling eyes and his granite countenance melted. "For you, anything," he said in a most tender, affection-filled voice. He gave her a quick peck on the temple. As he turned to Charlotte, his demeanor turned, too. "I'll see you later," he said, his tone cool.

Charlotte nodded, and much to her disgust and amazement, Tex whistled and Toto trotted happily out of the room after him.

"C'mon, pig." Tex settled onto a bench beneath a shade tree in the fenced-in training yard of his clinic. Legs spread, he propped his elbows on his knees and offered a slice of apple to Toto. The little pig eagerly mashed the apple between his teeth. Juice dribbled from his jowls as he nudged Tex for more.

Tex grinned and carved another chunk off the apple with his pocket knife. A hot breeze kicked up a bit of dust in the training yard, and off in the distance cattle bawled as they were herded from one pasture to the next. Overhead, some puffy clouds scudded, and Tex enjoyed the few moments of quiet in his otherwise hectic day.

Toto's moist snout quivered as he snuffed the air for the scent of apple. Tiny, watery eyes beseeching, his stare was fixed on Tex's hands. The greedy grunts that emanated low in his throat had Tex laughing out loud.

"You've got a sweet tooth. No wonder you don't like your new master. She's about as sour as they come." He chuckled at his joke and scratched the lip-smacking animal on his wiry head.

Charlotte Beauchamp.

What a piece of work. Just about as uppity as her name. Hard to believe she was related to Miss Clarise. He gave his head a slow shake. Whoever heard of leaving an animal in a car on a hot day like this? It was obvious she didn't have a lick of common sense.

Okay, so she'd taken precautions. He had to give her that. But still, anything could have gone wrong. Another hour and old Toto here would have been Totoast.

"Here you go." Tex reached into the bag that lay on the bench beside him, pulled out a second apple and deftly carved it in two.

With affection, Tex pushed the grizzly animal back to better pat and scratch his haunches. He loved all kinds of animals. Ugly, cute, big, little, they were all the same to him. He'd had this special affinity ever since he could remember. His mother still loved to tell the tale about how he'd tried to saddle and ride the family dog before he was out of diapers.

Tex had no patience for people who did not respect animals. Even a relative of Miss Clarise's. Even a very attractive relative of Miss Clarise's. One with thick, honey-brown hair and light blue eyes that snapped like fourth of July sparklers when she was mad, and legs that went on for…well, forever.

He'd gotten a pretty good view of those legs through that gauzy skirt of hers as she wrestled with the pig. In fact he might have been tempted to come to her aid a little sooner if it hadn't been for that awesome view.

Yeah, she was a looker all right. But looks meant nothing. In Tex's book, the measure of a human being was how they treated helpless creatures. Babies, senior citizens, the infirm and yes, even animals. Tex had a soft spot for them all. Right now, animals were his forte. He figured babies and seniors would follow in life's natural progression. If he was lucky.

As far as the cantankerous Charlotte Beauchamp was concerned, he'd just as soon leave Toto as ill-mannered as he was. Would serve her right. Spoiled rich girl. Never done a lick of work in her life.

Ah, well. For Miss Clarise's sake, he'd do the job and do it right.

"So." Tex sliced off another chunk of the apple for the pig. "You inherited Charlotte Beauchamp, huh?"

Toto snorted.

"Yeah, yeah. My sentiments, exactly."

Miss Clarise and Big Daddy watched through the parlor window as Charlotte strolled past the fountain in front of their antebellum mansion. Following their directions, she took the box-hedge lined path that led to the stables beyond.

"She's a spunky little thing," Big Daddy murmured from where he stood behind his wife, his hands on the gentle swell of her hips.

"She's a Beauchamp."

"Yeahup. Kinda reminds me of another purty little gal I know."

Miss Clarise turned in her husband's arms. "Oh, Big Daddy. You're still such a tease." With a gentle inclination of her head, she rested her nose against his. "Was it my imagination, or were there some sparks flying between those two?"

"Well, he's a Brubaker and she's a Beauchamp. I'd say they don't stand much of a chance."

"Mmm. I'm thinking an outdoor wedding."

"They do seem to like the luau theme."

"I'll begin making notes."

Chapter Two

Never in her life had Charlotte Beauchamp taken a more instant dislike to another human being than she had to Tex Brubaker. For her, it was hate at first sight.

Still fairly vibrating with indignation, Charlotte cursed the arrogant cowboy under her breath as she followed the path to the animal behavioral clinic behind the horse stables. How could such a lovable man as Big Daddy Brubaker have such a swine for a nephew?

No wonder Tex got on with animals so well.

He *was* one.

Right there in front of Big Daddy and Miss Clarise, he'd made her out to be some kind of evil—Charlotte's breathing grew rapid and she clenched her fists at the thought—animal murderer. Proclaimed her guilty until proven innocent. It had to be one of the singularly most mortifying moments of her life. While it was true she was not overly fond of Toto—or any animal for that matter—she'd never purposefully try to harm him. Twin flames licked her cheeks at the very thought.

Yes, Charlotte had made up her mind about old Tex-baby, all right. He was one of those bleeding heart "animals-are-people-too" weirdos who tried to get into the psyche of a squirrel or a snake or a snail, all in the name of science. Yeah, right. How many tax dollars were thrown away on that junk every year? she wondered.

Too bad Tex hadn't been born about eighty years sooner. The crotchety old Nanna Dorothy would have enjoyed his particular brand of animal magnetism.

He was offensive and arrogant and snotty.

But boy-howdy, as much as Charlotte hated to admit it, he was handsome. And all man. A woman would have to be dead not to notice those flashing sapphire eyes and that deep pair of dimples that seemed to run in the Brubaker family. He'd been wearing a cowboy hat, but from what she could tell, he had a full head of wavy dark hair that fell over his forehead in a most unruly, and thoroughly appealing manner.

And he was built, oh mama. His western shirt had been unbuttoned, revealing a snug T-shirt stretched over a powerful chest and a washboard stomach. His well-worn jeans fit like the proverbial glove and even his easy gait screamed a kind of sexy nonchalance.

Not that Charlotte cared.

He was a jerk.

Didn't matter what he looked like. He could be Elvis incarnate and it wouldn't make any difference.

In no particular hurry to see man—nor beast—she meandered at a tortoise's pace from the path to the tree-lined driveway, through the front pastures, past the stables and around back, to the modern and surprisingly impressive, Animal Behavioral Center.

For one very serious moment, she paused and contemplated simply turning on her heel and leaving. The very idea of having to face Tex now and listen to another smug lecture on the care and psychological handling of a pig was nearly as repugnant as picking up the horrible animal and making a home with him for the next however many years.

Surely, no amount of inheritance could be worth this hassle. Then again, Charlotte did enjoy the creature comforts.

Eating.

Bathing.

Shoes on her feet.

With a weary sigh, she lifted a hand and shaded her eyes against the glare of the midday sun. From where she stood, she could see both Tex and Toto sitting in some sort of fenced-in yard, getting on like a house on fire. Well, she guessed that made a kind of cosmic sense. Both were thoroughly ill-mannered.

With a radar inherent to canines, dogs of all breeds and sizes began to bark at her approach. Charlotte could only thank God that they were all locked in a series of tidy chain-link kennels. She disliked dogs nearly as much as she disliked pigs.

Tex glanced up and caught her standing there, looking at him from a grove of trees that shaded an area near the stables. He'd taken off his western shirt and wore the sleeves of his snug, cotton T-shirt pushed up over his steely biceps. Charlotte swallowed. She'd led a very sheltered, quiet life, taking care of Nanna Dorothy. The various handymen and male neighbors she came into contact with on a daily basis couldn't hold a candle to Tex, when it came to sheer male energy. It was nearly primal.

Animal.

No wonder he'd chosen this line of work. He was as

wild and uncontrolled as the unbroken horses that pranced and snorted in the paddock beyond.

As the dogs lunged and yapped against their chain-link enclosures, her gaze collided with his, and for a heart-stopping moment, Charlotte stood, trying to decide between fight or flight.

Without breaking the visual grip he held on her, Tex commanded the dogs to quiet down and, quite miraculously, they did.

She took a step back, seriously considering flight.

"So," he drawled, lifting his voice to be heard, "you think you can learn to handle a pig?"

Okay, fight it was.

Shoulders snapped back, head held high, she marched across the road and moved to the fence. She looked him in the eye with defiance. "Oh, yes," she answered, voice saccharine. "And Toto, too."

Begrudging dimples bracketed the sides of his pouty lips, revealing a flawless set of pearly whites.

Charlotte's heart gave a vicious kick beneath her ribs.

"Touché," he murmured. A flash of approval lit his eyes for a nanosecond. Inclining his head, he shifted a straw from one corner of his mouth to the other and indicated a gate to her left. "It's unlocked."

Charlotte followed the direction of his eyes and once inside the fence, noted that the area was sectioned into various training zones. Some were covered with asphalt, some with wood chips or gravel, some with grass. All kinds of equipment, obviously used for the purpose of dog obedience training lay scattered about, as if it had been hastily abandoned in favor of rescuing a sweltering swine.

Awkwardly, Charlotte moved to where Tex sat sprawled on a bench and, after hovering beneath his penetrating gaze for a moment, finally perched on the farthest corner.

"So. You're going to move into the big house, huh?"

She nodded. "Tomorrow."

He grunted.

"Your enthusiasm is underwhelming."

"No skin off my nose."

"Well that's something anyway."

"I'm going to obedience train your animal as a favor to Miss Clarise."

He made it sound like he'd rather amputate his head with a rusty razor blade.

"I'm under no illusions as to your motives."

"Good. So you won't be offended when I resign, after giving it the good old college try."

"Why would you resign?" She hoped her smirk conveyed the proper amount of superiority. Unable to resist, she taunted. "Don't think you can train a simple pig?"

"Not the pig I'm worried about." He shrugged and carved off another chunk of apple for the ravenous Toto. "I think the pig could learn fast and have a complete change of attitude in a remarkable amount of time."

"Then what?"

"You."

"Me?" Charlotte touched her fingertips to her throat and gave an incredulous little laugh. "Me what?"

"I don't think you have what it takes."

"You are talking in circles. I don't have what it takes to do what?"

"In order to make any real progress with a pet, the master needs a certain amount of training, too, or it's not even worth bothering. This will take a concerted effort on your part and I doubt that you have the time, talent or inclination."

"I don't have the time...talent..." she spat the words like bullets, "or inclination, but my *pig* does?"

Charlotte stared at him and groped for a scathing put-down. The audacity! Smile brittle, she drew a deep, cleansing breath.

"No offense," she lied, intending to carve his over-sized ego down to size, "but surely any moron can learn to handle a stupid animal."

Tex stared at her as if she'd just been belched from the southernmost bowels of Hades. "Stupid animal? You think animals are *stupid?*"

Gaze skyward, Charlotte dropped her shoulders. "Oh, great. Here we go."

"What's that supposed to mean?"

"I know your type. You're going to tell me how brilliant and sensitive my pig is."

"Lady, you don't know diddly-squat about me. And it's obvious you know nothing about animals, if you don't believe a pig is capable of thinking. Or feeling."

"Feeling?" Charlotte guffawed in a most unladylike fashion.

"Considering your attitude, I can see that it won't matter to you that your pig is suffering from depression, among other things."

Unable to hold back, Charlotte looked into his sober expression and burst out laughing. "Toto? Depressed? He's too mean to be depressed. Besides, what on earth does he have to be depressed about? All his life, he's lived in the lap of luxury. That pig has a better diet than most people."

"Be that as it may, this pig misses your late grand-mother Dorothy."

"Great-grandmother."

"Whatever."

"That's a bunch of pop-psychology hogwash. Forgive the pun."

Tex pulled the straw from the corner of his mouth and regarded her. "You're pretty sure of yourself, aren't you?"

Charlotte met his dark, probing gaze and suddenly wasn't sure of her own name. "Yes," she snapped, not even able to remember the question that she was yes-ing. Lawsy, he had beautiful eyes.

"Yep. That's what I thought." The crack of his hands slapping his thighs startled Toto. "As much as I hate to disappoint Miss Clarise, this isn't going to work. Why don't you take your pig now, and go back to wherever it is you came from and find someone else to help you with his behavior problems? I can't work with you."

"Fine." Charlotte stood and tossed her head. She didn't need this arrogant animal shrink. "Come on, Toto." Grabbing his leash, she dragged the reluctant pig, kicking and squealing, to the gate.

It was a battle she'd never forget as long as she lived. Dogs barked, ranch hands paused in their duties to stare and Tex, she was quite sure, was laughing up his sleeve.

It took her a full twenty minutes to wrestle Toto the fifty yards to her parked car and stuff him inside. It wasn't until she attempted to start her engine that she remembered Tex informing her that she'd run out of gas.

Hunt, Red and Fuzzy, three of Big Daddy's ranch hands had stared from the paddock as Charlotte struggled past. When she'd made it to her car, they'd moved to the fence and watched with interest, her wrestling match with the stubborn little pig.

"Shooie, baby," Hunt said, an appreciative grin causing the little lines at the corners of his eyes to fork. "Now there's a looker."

"Yep," Fuzzy teased, "the girl's not bad either."

"You get a gander at those legs?" Hunt poked a straw in his mouth and chewed it thoughtfully.

"Um-hm. Have to be blind and dead to miss 'em," Red put in.

"And all that curly, wild, honey-colored hair. Haven't seen anything like her around here for a long time." Resting his arms on the top rail of the fence, Hunt strained to see Charlotte as she disappeared inside her car. "And she's built, too. Did you get a load of that pair of—"

As he gestured to his chest, Red, blushing furiously, interrupted. "She must be a new client at the clinic."

"She's Miss Clarise's second cousin-once-removed." Tex ambled up behind them carrying a five-gallon gas can. "And don't let this book's cover fool ya, boys. She seems like a sweet little thing, but she's mean."

Hunt squinted as he nibbled his straw. "Take a real man to handle her, huh?"

"A real crazy man, sure. Why, Hunt? You think you're up for the job?"

"Could be."

"Yeah, well, don't get your fingers too near her mouth. She bites."

Hunt guffawed.

As Tex headed down the road to rescue this hellcat in distress, he was disturbed to note that Hunt's interest in Charlotte bothered him. Now, why should that bother him? Must be he felt protective over poor Hunt, he reasoned. Charlotte would have him for lunch.

Yeah. The guy that ended up with Charlotte Beauchamp, would have to be one tough customer.

* * *

Charlotte pounded the dashboard and shrieked in frustration.

"Why me?" she groaned, and allowed her head to drop against the steering wheel. She lifted her eyes and squinted through the windshield. Tex was approaching with a gas can and a self-satisfied smile.

A low, guttural growl emanated from her throat.

She would ignore him.

He could keep his blasted gas. She would sooner push her car back to Nanna's, than take charity from him.

Charlotte looked back toward the stables and scanned the surrounding area. What had happened to the rest of the ranch hands? Except for Tex, there suddenly wasn't another soul in sight.

Just her luck.

She muttered under her breath and sagged against the scalding upholstery of the driver's seat. She thought about asking Miss Clarise for help, but that didn't feel right. She was already imposing on her far too much as it was.

It seemed she was stuck with the arrogant Tex.

Charlotte exhaled heavily and closed her eyes. Lord have mercy, it was hot in this car. As much as she hated to admit it, Tex had been right. She unbuttoned the top button of her blouse and lifted her hair off the back of her neck. Too many minutes without the air conditioner and it would be curtains for sure. She was feeling faint already.

With that infuriatingly easy gate of his, Tex ambled to the car and set the gas can on the ground. Hand dangling, he draped a casual arm on the roof of her car and knocked on her window.

Much to Charlotte's chagrin, Toto squealed with delight. She sighed. Traitorous swine. Ignoring Tex would be impossible now. Especially with Toto clambering over her lap to plaster the window with affectionate snout prints. She lowered the window and tried to affect a breezy, nonchalant attitude. As if she enjoyed sitting in a sauna with a rapturous hundred-plus-pound-pig dancing on her thighs.

His brow cocked in a rakish fashion, he leaned forward. "Need some help?"

Charlotte opened her door and struggled to get out from under Toto, who was eager to once again be rescued by his knight in shining armor.

"C'mon, boy," Tex said, and lifted the animal off Charlotte's lap as easily as if he'd been a pillow and stowed the wriggling beast on the ground. Then, before Charlotte had a chance to disembark, he thrust his head into the car and began to look around.

"Excuse me!" Charlotte reared back as his thick, dark hair brushed her knees and he began to grope under her seat. "What... Stop! What are you..." she gasped, "are you trying to look up my skirt?"

A cross between a grunt and a snort rumbled from his belly. "Dream on, cousin," he said, his hot breath fanning her calves. With a roguish arch of the brow, he continued his search and then, finally finding what he was looking for, he tugged on the release lever to her gas cap. The muscles in his arms flexed as he pushed himself up and brought his nose within inches of hers. "The sooner we get you on the road, the better, no?"

Charlotte smiled sweetly. "Absolutely."

"Right." With one smooth move, he levered off the seat and snagging the gas can, sauntered to the rear of her car. Toto followed him like a docile puppy.

Peeling herself from the upholstery, Charlotte got out of the car and tried to appear disinterested in the way the muscles in his back rippled as he effortlessly hefted the gas can and began to fill her tank.

"This ought to be enough gas to get you to the nearest filling station."

Charlotte crossed her arms under her breasts. He didn't need to sound quite so eager to get rid of her. "Yes. We are anxious to be on our way."

"Good."

Brow furrowed, she ground her back teeth. And he taught manners to animals?

Toto flopped down and sprawled out on top of Tex's booted feet. Tex didn't seem to notice.

She lifted her arms up over her forehead and squinted at the shimmering horizon. The humidity was unbearable. Shifting her gaze to the Brubakers' main house, she could see rows of pillars, like sturdy sentinels, guarding the huge antebellum mansion's front porch and supporting the ornate second-floor veranda. The fantastically long driveway was lined with shade trees and a half-dozen other buildings dotted the surrounding area. Servants' quarters, a giant garage, a gazebo, a greenhouse, the expansive stables and Behavioral Center, endless acres of formal gardens complete with all manner of fountains, ponds, statuary and piped in music. It was a magical world.

And, though Nanna Dorothy had been wealthy, her home was nothing compared to this palatial estate.

Behind the house, Charlotte knew there was a sparkling blue Olympic-sized pool. *Oh,* she sighed and could feel a trickle of sweat skittering down her spine, *how tempting.* She glanced down at Toto. First thing tomorrow, she was going to don her swimsuit and plunge into that pool. That is, if she could find some poor soul to baby-sit her pig for an hour or two.

She lowered her arms and wrapped them around her waist. For all intents and purposes, she was a single mother. The single mother of Rosemary's baby.

Angling her head, she peeked at Tex's rugged features as he concentrated on filling her tank.

She'd blown it.

There wasn't another animal behaviorist in these parts for miles. Without his expertise, she could look forward to who knew how many years living with the crazed Toto. She glanced into her back seat, at the shredded seat cover, and her shoulders sagged.

Without proper training, Toto would certainly end up next to a stack of pancakes down at Ned's Lonestar grill, and Charlotte would have to forgo her inheritance in favor of life on the street. She was caught between a pig— her eyes followed the hills and valleys that strained beneath the cotton of Tex's T-shirt—and a hard place.

Perhaps it was time to swallow her pride.

Tex stood and set the can on the ground. As he twisted her car's gas cap firmly back into place, Charlotte took a tentative step forward.

"Thanks," she murmured, feeling suddenly bashful.

"No big deal."

"Well, thanks anyway." She glanced up into his face, trying to get a bead on his attitude, but his gaze was shuttered. Touching her tongue to her lips, she decided a direct approach with this man would probably be her best bet. "Uh, Tex?"

"Huh?"

"Do you really think that Toto can be helped?"

Before he answered, Tex put the top back on the empty gas can, then straightened and looked her directly in the eye. "He's basically a good animal. Spoiled. Feeling a little displaced without his original master, but I think he could be okay. It would take some doing, but he can be helped, yes."

"Look, since I'm going to be living here for a while, do you think you might change your mind and take Toto—" she cleared her throat and glanced at the ground "—and me, on as clients? As a favor to Miss Clarise? I promise I'll…you know…help out and stuff."

His lip drew into a skeptical curl. "You're willing to make whatever effort it takes?"

"Sure." Whatever effort it took on her part couldn't be that hard. One, maybe two lessons ought to do the trick.

And, when they were done each day, maybe she could head out to the pool and completely relax, for the first time in ten years. Serene in the knowledge that she was finally off duty. Not at anyone's constant beck and call.

"Okay," he said, much to her surprise. "You're moving in tomorrow, right?"

"Yes."

"Morning?"

"Yes."

"Good. Then I'll expect you down here and ready to work at ten."

"Ten? But I won't even be—"

"You can unpack later. I have a training appointment open at ten." He nudged Toto off his feet and with a curt nod picked up his gas can and sauntered off.

"But I—"

"Ten."

Mouth ajar, Charlotte stared after him. He had to be the rudest, most arrogant jerk she'd ever had the misfortune to meet.

The next morning, Tex stood at the glass wall of windows in the Brubaker kitchen drinking coffee and watching as Charlotte attempted to unload Toto from the back of her car. The butler on duty at the Circle BO, along with two assistants had already disappeared into the mansion with the bulk of her belongings, leaving Charlotte alone to struggle with her pig.

Tex grinned over the rim of his coffee cup. Wheelbarrow style, she had the pig's back legs in her hands. For every few inches she managed to eke the stubborn animal out of her car, he would claw his way—squealing all the while—back inside, and then some. Slowly, but surely, Charlotte was being sucked into her car.

"Good boy," Tex murmured into his cup, before taking a healthy slug of steaming java. "Take her back to where she came from."

The last thing Tex needed was another stiff-necked owner expecting him to do all the work while she filed her nails and looked on with disinterest. He knew the type. Had to work with them all the time.

And, though Charlotte hadn't exactly signed up for Toto, she was the animal's master for better or worse. Her keen disdain for the poor pig was only going to make matters more difficult. First thing he needed to deal with was an attitude adjustment on her part.

It was much more work than he needed, especially at this busy juncture in his career. Why had he agreed to meet with her at ten, this morning? He glanced at the clock and groaned into his coffee cup. Nine forty-five. He knew why.

Long, shapely legs and a sassy little mouth, that's why he'd agreed to work with her. She was a pain in the neck, he could tell already. But, there was something about Charlotte. Something he couldn't quite put his finger on. Something that was worth discovering.

Having wriggled back out of the car, Charlotte was now standing, arms akimbo, and shouting at her pig. Eyes blazing, she gave her head a defiant toss, flinging her unruly mop of wonderful hair out of her face and let go with a string of sizzling expletives that should have had Toto's haunches turning to bacon.

Her voice, usually sultry and refined, reached Tex through the pane of glass. "Come out of there this instant, you miserable tub of lard! You seem to forget that I enjoy the 'other white meat'! Stinking swine! Get out of there right now or I swear I'll have you for dinner!"

Toto reared back and squealed in such a way that he seemed to be laughing.

A surge of pity—for the woman or the pig, he couldn't decide—had Tex stepping away from the window. He poured a second cup of coffee for Charlotte, tucked an apple in his shirt pocket and headed out the kitchen's side door to the circular drive, a cup in each hand.

"Need some help?" he asked as he approached the frazzled Charlotte.

"No!" she shouted, then took a deep breath and stretched her lips into a pseudo-smile. She waved at him with an airy hand. "No, thank you."

He had to give her credit. Her prim, breezy demeanor made it sound as if battling a pig out of her car were no big deal.

"Coffee?" He held out the cup he'd poured for her.

For an instant, she hesitated then held out her hand. "Yes, thanks." She sounded anything but grateful.

She hated him. For some strange reason, that made him grin. "It's strong and black."

"I take cream and sugar." Lips puckered, she blew across the rim and took a sip. Tex stared, mesmerized.

"But I guess this'll do. At least it'll give me the energy I need to show this pig who's boss."

Tex gave his head a clearing shake. It was difficult to tell if she was talking about him, or Toto. "You're going to need some lessons first."

"Oh, for pity's sake. Right." Her shoulders sagged as she glanced at her watch. "It's almost ten. I suppose we should get started?"

Tex nodded. She didn't sound exactly eager, but he supposed that was to be expected. With a snap of his fingers, Toto bounded out of her car and sat adoringly upon his feet.

A droll expression on her face, Charlotte turned to him, eyes narrowed. "How did you do that?"

"You'll find out in lesson six."

"*Six?* You mean there are more than one or two lessons?"

"If you want your pig to eventually obey you, you are going to have to work at this for one or two months."

"*Months?*" Her jaw dropped. "You've got to be kidding!"

"Nope."

"But I'm not even going to be living here that long. I'm going to go find a job, and move out."

"Excellent."

"Gee, thanks."

He ignored her sarcasm. "Until then, you are going to have to work with your pig every day. After you move out, you can commute."

In a petulant gesture, Charlotte stamped her foot and stared at him. "Commute? With this pig? No way! I want you to fix him, and fix him fast! I thought you were a big-time animal shrink."

"Behaviorist. I study the behavior of animals, mainly

dogs and horses and some large farm animals." He inclined his head at the pig who sat patiently on his foot. "Toto here qualifies." The bristly fur on Toto's head made a pleasant scratching sound against his pant leg as the pig nuzzled him for attention.

Tex pulled the apple and a penknife out of his shirt pocket and carved a chunk off for the pig.

"What's so interesting about the behavior of horses and dogs?"

"Well, for one thing, my clinic's research allows the development of new training methods that help improve the efficiency of working cattle ranches like the Circle BO. And, even though most good-sized ranches are becoming more dependent on machinery to herd cattle," he said, running a hand over his chest and gesturing toward the stables with his coffee cup, "horses and dogs can go anywhere. They will always be needed on a cattle ranch. Sometimes, depending on a good horse or dog can mean the difference between life and death. You know," he pointed to Toto, "there are some pigs who have been known to save a person's life in an emergency."

Charlotte shot a skeptical look at Toto. "If you say so."

"C'mon. Let's go to the training yard and we can get started."

Tex noticed she held the coffee mug in such a death grip her knuckles had turned white. They went down the driveway and then crossed to the path that cut through the formal gardens. From there, they traversed the sprawling lawn and headed toward the stables. Curly tail bouncing, Toto trotted alongside. He was clearly in hog heaven as he sniffed and grunted and paused occasionally to fling dirt into the air with his snout.

Still sensing a great deal of animosity from her camp,

Tex attempted to keep their conversation on a light, business level. Maybe she would loosen up with time. At least he hoped so.

"So what do you know about pigs?" he asked, glancing in her direction.

She bunched and dropped her shoulders. "They're great with chutney or a honey glaze."

"Other than that, is there anything you'd like to know about your animal?"

"Yes. How long is he going to live?"

Tex grinned. She was single-minded. Changing her attitude toward the spunky little Toto was going to be tough. "The average life expectancy of a potbellied pig, like Toto here, is anywhere from twelve to eighteen years."

"You're *kidding!*" Her mouth sagged open.

"Nope. Longer, if you take good care of him."

"*Oh, no.*" Charlotte stopped in her tracks and buried her face in her hands.

"What's wrong?"

She moaned and peered at him from between her fingers. "Toto is only three years old. That means I'm stuck with him for the next nine to fifteen years!"

Tex threw back his head and let the laughter flow. That was a riot. Miss Uppity-Thing here, had to give the best years of her life to a pig. Wonderful. It would do her some good. Obviously, she'd led a pampered life up till now. Owning this pig would build some much-needed character.

Stunned, Charlotte began to move woodenly after him. "I'll be over *forty* by the time he finally decides to kick off!"

Tears welled in Tex's eyes and he had to pause and slap his thighs for a minute.

"It's not funny," she snapped and dragged her hair away from her blazing gaze.

"Right, right." Tex dabbed at his cheeks with his sleeves. Priceless. This moment was priceless. Inhaling deeply, he rubbed his cheeks and struggled to gain control. However, try as he might, he could not wipe the grin from his face. "Considering that you and Toto are going to be roommates for a while, is there anything else you'd like to know?"

"No!"

Tex hooted. He couldn't look at her beet-red face. It was all just too funny. "Okay," he said carefully, "I'll just fill you in some of the high points. Let's see. Toto has a highly developed sense of smell."

"I'll say," she grumbled. "Smells like hobo socks."

"No. I don't mean that he stinks. I mean that he can smell very well. His snout is longer than a domestic pig's. He can smell things that you and I can't smell."

"How can he stand himself?"

"Pigs don't mind pungent odors."

Charlotte groaned, and again, Tex had to fight the mirth he felt rising in his throat.

"Also, it might be helpful to know that Toto has very poor eyesight. Pigs are clean, very smart and good-natured. If you feed him correctly, he should top out at about a hundred and twenty-five pounds."

"Great," Charlotte deadpanned. "We can share clothes."

Laughter bubbled into Tex's throat, and this time he did nothing to stop it. She might be a pain in the neck, but she was funny.

Together they crossed the road to the stables, and rounded the paddock where two frisky colts gamboled.

Charlotte, Tex noticed, didn't even spare the fuzzy babes a glance.

A slight pang niggled in his gut.

She really wasn't an animal person. Too bad. It was rare that he met someone, especially a woman, who didn't fawn over a couple of wobbly legged colts. He knew there were animal people. And he knew there were people people. Tex liked to think there was room in his heart for both people and animals. Pets were the spice of life. Man's best friend.

However not, apparently, in all cases. Toto stopped and flung a dirt clod back at Charlotte. Her indignant gasp had Tex biting his cheek once again.

Tex opened the gate to the training arena and led Charlotte and Toto to the back door of his offices.

He flipped on the lights and motioned for Charlotte to take one of the two club chairs situated in front of his cluttered desk. Toto followed as he strode to a bookcase. His office was as disheveled as his desk, stuffed with cages and equipment and large bags of rawhide chew toys and pet food. Bookshelves lined the walls, floor to ceiling, and in one corner, a television and VCR were housed in a cabinet crammed with videos on the subject of animal behavior and training methods. In spite of the chaos, the room was clean and modern and Tex loved this world he'd built over the last year.

Chin to shoulder, he glanced back at Charlotte. "I ask all of my clients to do some reading and a little study as part of the training process."

"Study?" Charlotte's heavy exhale denoted her reluctance to become involved.

Tex chose to ignore it. "Yeah. Usually I assign a text or two on the breed of the dog or horse, and then several books on the subject of obedience and training. But,'' he paused and scanned his shelves, ''since you have a pig...''

He scratched his head. What did he do with those books on pigs? Oh, right. He crossed to an antique pie-safe near the wall behind Charlotte and began shuffling through great piles of periodicals and other odds and ends.

''Here we go.'' Triumphant, he held up three books, several trade magazines and periodicals and a work-book. He kicked the doors to the pie-safe shut before the contents could slide out to the floor. Moving to Charlotte's side, he dumped the books in her lap. ''Happy reading.''

Charlotte held up the first title. ''Think Like a Pig.'' She looked askance at Tex. ''Obviously, you've read this one.''

He rolled his eyes, choosing not to dignify her barbs with a retort. ''It's a good book. That one, and the one on care and feeding are excellent.''

''Which one?'' She sorted through her stack. ''Eat Like a Pig?''

''Scoff if you will. If you just give it half a chance, before you know it, you and Toto will be inseparable.''

''Dare I dream?''

Tex moved behind his desk and sinking to his chair, regarded her. ''It could happen.''

''Why does that make me want to cry?''

''What have you got against animals?''

''Nothing. Do I have to have one for a roommate?''

''They say people who have pets live longer.''

''I'm sure the reverse is true in my case.''

''You know, you're going to have to commit to mak-

ing some serious changes to seeing Toto in a new light."
At the sound of his name, the little pig made a series of
little grunting noises and rubbed his head against Tex's
shin. "You're going to have to work very closely with
me for a long time."

Charlotte flashed a glance at him and pulled her lower
lip between her teeth. The color in her cheeks was high
and she looked rattled. Had he been too blunt with her?
It was clear she abhorred the idea.

"Can you do that?" he pressed.

She nodded. "I guess I have no choice."

"Good. Then let's get started."

As Tex stood, the door to his office opened and his
intern, a veterinary student from a nearby university,
stepped through. Upon spying Charlotte, the man
glanced at Tex, and then ran a hand over his thinning
pate. He shuffled forward and held out his hand to Charlotte.

"Hi." An agitated honking issued forth from his generous nostrils. "I'm Wally, Tex's intern and part-time
research assistant. You must be the ten o'clock appointment."

There was something about the slightly predatory look
on Wally's face that put Tex off. Not that *he* had—or
wanted—any proprietary claim on Charlotte, but still, it
seemed unprofessional on Wally's part.

Charlotte smile politely and took the intern's hand.
"How do you do. I'm Charlotte Beauchamp, pig owner,
shirttail relative."

"Ah." Wally's smile broadened, pushing his cheeks
up to knock his glasses off-kilter. He stuffed his shirt into
his sagging corduroys and hauled his belt back up.
"Well, any relative of the Brubakers' is a relative of

mine.'' More grating laughter echoed about the room.

Feeling suddenly irritable, Tex pulled Charlotte's hand from Wally's, and hustled her to the door. "Okay. Now that introductions are out of the way, let's get to work. Wally, clean up in here, will ya?"

Chapter Three

"Toto, stay." Slowly, Tex backed away from where the pig sat on a patch of grass in the training area. When he'd achieved about a ten-foot space between himself and the animal, he stopped.

Snout quivering, Toto snorted and looked quizzically at the man.

Tex withdrew a baby carrot from a plastic bag and held it up. "Toto, come here."

Charlotte watched as Toto trotted obediently to Tex and took the carrot. They'd been working on this particular trick for twenty minutes and—after over an hour of variations on this and other mundane exercises—she was growing weary. How long, in heaven's name, did it take a pig to learn something as simple as coming when called? Tex, she noted sourly, didn't seem the least bit tired of this sport and insisted on educating her, as well as the pig.

"Pigs learn very rapidly, if you teach them properly."

"Oh. Umm. I see that." Charlotte yawned.

"The reward system works well when training all animals. Including humans. This is nothing new."

No kidding.

"Here." Tex offered her the bag of baby carrots. "Your turn. I think he understands the basic principle now."

"You think?" Charlotte held out her hand and took the bag.

Man, she was tired. She'd only gotten two hours of sleep last night after staying up late to pack up Nanna Dorothy's house. Then after falling face first into bed, Toto-the-terrible kept her awake by making the most incredible racket. When he wasn't grunting and groaning, he was up rooting around and slamming into her mattress with his head.

To clear away the cobwebs, she took a deep breath and forced herself to concentrate.

"How goes the training?" a masculine voice called from beyond the chain-link fence.

Charlotte angled her head to see one of the younger— and very handsome—ranch hands watching. She wondered how long he'd been standing there.

"It's goin'." Tex was noncommittal and obviously irritated at being interrupted. "What do you want, Hunt?"

"Nothin'. Just thought I'd stop by to see how y'all are doin'."

Charlotte was glad for the distraction. "Terrible," she confessed, immediately liking this cowboy's affable charm. Why couldn't Tex be as personable? It certainly wouldn't kill him to take a little break, would it? She straightened and turned her back on Tex. "I don't think we're getting anywhere."

"And we won't, if you don't pay attention," Tex grumbled.

She took a step toward the man Tex referred to as Hunt. "You work here?"

"Yep. When I'm not flirting with pretty girls." Hunt's eyes twinkled.

She laughed. Something about him made Charlotte feel like a kid again. He was really a cutie-pie. She wanted to explore a conversation with Hunt, but sensed Tex's glacial stare from behind.

Tex cleared his throat.

"Sounds like the boss is callin' ya." Hunt chuckled. "I'd better git, before he throws me out of here." He winked. "I'll see you around?"

"That might be nice." Wistfully, Charlotte watched him go. Hunt would be an excellent distraction from the idiotic feelings of attraction she was fighting toward Tex. Tex was all wrong for her, that much was crystal-clear to them both. And Hunt had a sense of humor. Unlike some other people she knew.

"Come on, let's get back to work."

She turned to find Tex standing legs spread, arms folded across his chest and a scowl marring his rugged Brubaker face.

"Okay, okay." With a noisy huff, she stalked back to where he stood.

He pointed at the bag she still held in her hands. "Get a carrot and hold it out between your fingertips." His hand brushed against hers as he dug one out and demonstrated. "Like this. That way he can easily see it and get to it. I know this seems like common sense, but as we move along in our training, you'll see that it's much more involved than that.

"It's about positive versus negative reinforcement as well as gaining an understanding of how your animal's mind works. Your pet will respond to you much more rapidly, once you make him understand that you are interested in rewarding him for every good behavior. Part of the problem, I'm guessing, is that you have not been rewarding Toto for good behavior."

She cast him a droll glance. "What good behavior?"

Tex filled his lungs through his nose and slowly let the air out from between his teeth. "Okay. Go ahead and back up. No. Not that fast. Slow. Like this." With a gentle touch, he took her arm and guided her ten paces away from the patiently sitting pig. "Say 'stay' firmly one time, as you move back."

It was hard to think with him so close. Lips pursed, she blinked hard and did her best to focus on the pig.

"Staaaaayeee," she warned. Toto shifted on his haunches. "Stay! *Stay!*"

"All right already. I think he gets the picture. Remember, pigs are very intelligent. You don't need to threaten him."

"I wasn't threatening him. He was trying to get away."

"He was not. He was simply getting comfortable."

Though she suspected that he was laughing at her, and not with her, the sexy rumble further flustered her.

"C'mon. Let's start over."

Tex took her by the elbow and propelled her back to the starting point. An unwanted current of attraction ran directly from her elbow to the pit of her stomach, then spread in a warm flush up to her chest, then to her neck and on to her cheeks, where it settled and burned like a Texas grass fire.

Suddenly, the air seemed thicker, harder to breathe. Her heartbeat kicked up a notch, and a dull, oceanlike roar filled her ears.

All this, from a silly touch on the arm. How ridiculous.

Did he feel it, too?

She was too embarrassed to chance a glance directly at him, but could see the grim set of his jaw in her peripheral vision.

No, she decided, he didn't feel anything for her but politely schooled contempt. Disgusted with herself for allowing his maddening brand of macho charm to get under her skin, Charlotte tugged her elbow from his hand and took a step away. For his benefit she conjured up a smile, then rotated her shoulders.

"Try again," he urged.

She did. And, once again, Charlotte knew her retreat from the pig was probably too rapid, but wanted to get away from them both as quickly as possible. "Stay. Stay," she commanded, more to Tex than to the pig.

"No." Frustrated, Tex raked a hand over his shadowed jaw. "Say it once. And you have to slow down. Let's try again."

This time he took her by both elbows, pulled her against the solid wall of his body, and began to lead her away from Toto.

"First say 'Toto, stay.' Then—" he lowered his voice and his breath tickled the flyaway hairs that had fallen loose from her ponytail "—back up, slooow. See? Like this. Now, hold out his food and say, 'Toto, come here.'"

"Toto, come here," she commanded. Her voice sounded ridiculously breathy. Whether from the too-warm feel of him being so near, or from exhaustion with this tiresome chore, she couldn't be sure. Whatever the reason, she commanded herself to ignore his sparky touch. He was an animal person and she wasn't going to go and get a crush on him now, just because he had darling dimples and smelled of manly soap and had a body like some Greek statue.

Toto did not move.

"See? He hates me," she sighed.

"He does not hate you. He's just not used to you giving him a reward. Hold the carrot up higher—" he slid his hand down her arm to her wrist, urging her to follow his instructions "—where he can better see it, and try again."

A telltale trail of gooseflesh raced after his touch. Cheeks puffing in exasperation, Charlotte flung her hand out toward the pig.

Momentum thus created, the carrot slipped from her fingertips and sailed ten rapid paces to strike Toto between the eyes. The pig recoiled and ran in circles, squealing.

Tex plowed a hand through his hair. "Well, that oughta set things back a lesson or two."

She bit her lip. "Shall we take a break?"

He sighed. "Yeah. We're done." To Toto he offered a carrot and said, "Toto, come here."

The pig docilely obeyed and looked up at Tex with a dazed expression. "She didn't mean it, old boy. Just be patient. We'll get her whipped into shape pretty soon."

Charlotte took a giant step back. Away from Tex. Away from the constant current that seemed to buzz between them whenever she got too close. Feeling awkward, she stretched her arms out in front of her and twisted her fingers together.

"I've got to go. Um, listen. I need to run into Hidden Valley and start applying for jobs. You're sure you don't mind Toto staying here in one of your little, er—" she gestured toward the dogs "—cages while we're living here? I can't really take him with me to an interview and the sooner I get a job, the sooner I can get a place of my own. Plus, I'm sure Miss Clarise wouldn't want him running amuck in her house the way he did at Nanna Dorothy's."

"Yeah, he can stay here." Head slowly bobbing, Tex squinted off into the distance. "Whatever I can do to get you on your feet and on your own, consider it done. Let me know if I can help you with your resume, or give you a reference or help you pack, whatever."

"Perhaps you can help me pack, once I've had the chance to *un*pack."

At least he had the common decency to look somewhat abashed, she thought, feeling wounded.

"Of course."

She was spared having to force further idle parting chitchat as Wally chose that moment to step out of the office.

"How'd it go?" he inquired, too loudly, too jovially. If a bulldozer could swagger, it would walk like Wally, Charlotte was sure.

"Fine," she fibbed, not wishing to delve into her litany of failures at the moment.

"It'll take time," Tex told him, "but we'll get there."

Though Wally spoke to Charlotte, his eyes, she couldn't help but notice, landed everywhere on her person but her face. "I've been working on some shortcut training methods in my research. Maybe in your spare time, you'd like to try what I call 'rapid-progression' training."

Shortcut? That sounded appealing to Charlotte. Anything to get Toto's behavior acceptable in the shortest time possible.

"Okay. Sure. Sounds good. The sooner we get Toto trained, the sooner I can move on with my life. Speaking of which—" she lifted her hand in a casual goodbye salute and began to walk backward ''—I have to go see about getting a job. I'll talk to you both later.''

Wally nodded, and without another glance in Tex's direction, Charlotte made good her escape.

''She's a hotsy-totsy.'' Wally's gaze was riveted to Charlotte's shapely calves as she skipped off toward the main house. Tex watched the dopey grin stretch across Wally's face and could fairly see the saliva dripping from his incisors.

''Don't you have something you should be doing?''

''Yeah, but I needed a babe break.''

''Were you born without manners, or is it something you have to work at?'' Tex asked, his tone sardonic.

Nostrils flaring, Wally honked his amusement and tugged at his sagging pants. ''Relative or not, you can't tell me you haven't noticed that she's a dish.''

''We're not related.''

''But she said—''

''Wally, the university is not grading you to ogle the female clients. Show's over. Get on the Internet, and find out what you can on the care and handling of potbellied pigs. I need to bone up. And then you can get started on that research article you're supposed to write before the end of the term for my conference.''

''But it's not due till—''

''Change of plans. It's due next week, and the word count's been doubled.''

''*Doubled?*''

''Yep. Better get started. You're going to be burning the midnight oil, as it is.''

''Yeah, boss.'' Wally loped back to the office and Tex turned his attention to Charlotte's retreating form as she moved through the formal gardens and headed to the circular drive.

Something about the way Wally had come on to Charlotte irritated Tex. He was going to have to have a talk with that guy. Clients were off-limits.

Which was just as well for all concerned. Himself included.

Hopefully the attraction that seemed to crackle between Charlotte and himself was only a product of his overactive imagination. In silence, he berated himself for standing so close to her and touching her the way he had during their training session. He couldn't let that happen again. It was unprofessional. And dangerous. Already, he knew that he was developing a more than cursory interest in Charlotte.

Even now, just thinking of her conjured up images of the fragrance of her hair and the feel of her body pressed lightly against his as they worked. These echoes of her vital presence filled his mind, and caused his blood to pound and his gut to tighten. Wally was right. She was something.

When she wasn't talking.

Tex sighed and pressing his fingers to his brow, rubbed in soothing circles. The last thing he needed to do was get involved with a client. Especially one who felt about his line of work the way Charlotte did.

Eyes glazing over, he thought back to the last time he'd made the mistake of falling for a woman who wasn't an animal lover. But Jennifer was different than Charlotte in that she didn't exactly hate animals, she was simply allergic. To all animals. With the possible exception of aquatic life, Jennifer would cough and sneeze and get all blotchy and red in the face and swell up like a blowfish every time she came near an animal. And, if he'd been working closely with a dog or horse, Jennifer would even have the same reaction to him.

It was frustrating for them both, to say the least. Tex had wanted nothing more than to share his love for his work with Jennifer, but she was simply not able. Eventually, this became such a bone of contention, that they drifted apart.

If he was stupid enough to let his raging libido take control and get cozy with Charlotte, the same exact thing would happen for sure. He couldn't put himself through that wringer again. He wouldn't. One broken relationship for the year was plenty to his way of thinking.

The next woman he fell for was going to have a real affinity for not only him, but for the animals who made up who he was. His motto since Jennifer was: Love me, love my work.

Yep. For sanity's sake, he'd have to keep the luscious Charlotte at arms' length.

Charlotte returned to the Circle BO that afternoon somewhat deflated, but not defeated. So she hadn't exactly wowed 'em with her job history down there in old Hidden Valley. Seemed that changing bedpans and spoon-feeding chicken soup were not two of the requirements needed for pumping gas or slinging hash.

Not to worry, Charlotte told herself, as she changed out of her light linen summer suit and into a French-cut, one-piece black swimsuit. It was only her first day of the job search. She was not one to be easily daunted. She'd find something. Eventually. As of today, she'd only approached, and been turned down by, five or six businesses. There were still at least thirty or forty to go. Surely someone in Hidden Valley would need her unique blend of skills.

Bending at the waist, Charlotte flopped forward and gathered her hair in a pile at the crown of her head. A claw clip twisted the mass of curls into place. On her way out the door, she snagged her dark glasses, a towel and a fashion magazine.

It had been a grueling day. A brisk swim and then reclining on a lounge chair in the saunalike Texas heat would be wonderful therapy. In the past ten years spent taking care of Nanna Dorothy, such a treat had been a rarity indeed.

Tex watched Charlotte briskly run a towel over her hair. Then she settled back into the lounge chair that was situated under the lanai at the pool's edge. Picking up a magazine, she began to read.

From where Tex stood enjoying a frosty, after-work beer in his uncle's kitchen, he could make out that pair of shapely legs he'd so admired when they'd met the first time. He hung an arm on the massive window casing and enjoyed the distant view.

She was alone in the pool area.

All the Brubaker boys and the ranch hands were out on the range, Big Daddy and Miss Clarise had a party in Dallas, and aside from the servants, he was the only other person around. He knew he should head to his place, a small, two-man bunkhouse he shared with his cousin Kenny a mile or two beyond the stables, but the sight of her beautiful body, reclining so languidly in the shade kept him riveted to the spot.

He wondered if she'd had any luck finding a job. He hadn't been in the office when she'd come to check on Toto but he'd heard from Wally that she looked delicious in a skirt. Again, an irrational pang of something akin to jealousy seared his gut.

Jealousy?

Nah.

Of what? Charlotte and Wally? Charlotte and Hunt? His hollow laughter bounced back at him from the window pane.

No, it wasn't jealousy, he decided, now that he stopped to analyze it. It was…it was…ah, criminy. He didn't know what the hell it was. Whatever it was, he'd better get a grip on it before it got the best of him. As he took a long pull on his bottle, he noticed movement near the pool.

Wally?

Eyes narrow, jaw grim, Tex watched as the young intern let himself into the pool area through the wrought-iron gates. What was he still doing here? Wasn't he supposed to have classes all evening? And what about that paper he was writing?

Wally stood at the edge of the pool for a moment, gazing at the water and pretending not to notice Charlotte in the shadows of the lanai.

The set of his jaw was grim as Tex pushed off the window casing and strode to the door. Time to impress the client rules upon the intern.

Tex could hear their voices as he moved through the rose gardens and around the side of the pool house. He paused for a moment to listen. From where Tex stood, he could see Wally lumbering toward Charlotte. His nasal honking was meant to connote surprise.

"Charlotte! I didn't know you'd be out here."

"Bull," Tex muttered and rolled his eyes.

"Oh, hi, Wally." Charlotte sat up and pushed her sunglasses higher on the bridge of her nose.

"Mind if I join you?"

"I…uh, no. No, that's fine."

"Great. Hey, I'm glad I caught you." Wally propped a foot on a neighboring chair. Tone confidential, he leaned forward on his knee. "I wanted to talk to you about us working together with your pet. I think I have some cutting-edge training techniques that Tex may not have. Don't get me wrong, Tex is a good animal trainer and everything, but I'm onto a somewhat different approach."

Brows arched, Tex settled in to listen. This was getting interesting.

"What's different about your approach?"

"It's in the special rapid-progression system I'm developing to communicate with, and train animals." There was a mysterious quality to his voice.

"Really?"

"Yup." Straightening, Wally's chest puffed with self-importance. It was clear he was enjoying the attention of a beautiful woman. "Yeah, for years, man has been using sign language and the spoken word to communicate with animals. But I feel this is too restrictive. And slow."

"Oh?"

"Yes. In the wild, most animals operate under a social hierarchy within their species. Through silent communication, they can immediately make their position within their 'clan'—if you will—known. Not to mention when they should hunt, where they should migrate and of course, when they should mate."

Wally pinned her with a deep, probing stare.

"Oh."

"Right now, my research centers around proving my..." he lowered his voice "...*unique* theory based on this premise."

"What exactly is your unique theory?"

Wally glanced around, as if to make sure that no one

was eavesdropping. "I think it's possible to communicate with animals by using sustained eye contact and thinking your message into their minds."

"*Thinking* my message into Toto's mind?"

"I know this is going to sound weird." Wally's nervous laughter trumpeted forth from his nostrils like a donkey's bray. "But I believe that you can communicate with dogs, and maybe even your pig this way. In essence, I believe you can learn to speak pig."

Tex heaved an inward groan as he watched Wally fix Charlotte with his quixotic gaze. It was obvious he was trying to put his theory into practice getting her to pick up the signals he exuded.

How Tex's clinic had come to be the unfortunate recipient of the "meatball intern"—as Wally was known in the university's veterinary circle—continued to boggle his mind. Wally had been passed around from clinic to clinic for years as he pursued his various degrees. Luckily the assignment would only last a term, but still, working with this loose cannon was presenting its challenges.

"I...can...learn...to...speak...pig." Charlotte slowly repeated the words, as if trying to decide if this guy was for real or not.

"Silently."

"Silently?" She looked at him, over the top of her sunglasses.

"Yes. And, perhaps someday aloud."

"Aloud, as in...snorting?"

Tex battled a wave of laughter.

"Yes. I really think I'm on to something big, that someday humans may be able to use as well. A type of primal telepathy. We humans only use about one fifth of our brain capacity."

"Some more than others," Tex muttered.

"I think if we can tap into the other four-fifths—"

Tex snorted. "I think you've tapped one too many fifths already, buddy," he murmured.

"We would be amazed at the power we hold within. Anyway, in regard to animals, I'm writing an article on this theory and I'd like to test it out on a pig. On your pig. With you." Never breaking his meaningful eye contact with Charlotte, he nervously rearranged the longish hairs that were meant to cover his balding patch.

Caught off guard, Charlotte groped for a way out. "I...I..."

As much as he was enjoying the show, Tex couldn't stand there and let Wally foist his rather avant-garde ideas on Charlotte all evening. Even if she was a pain in the neck.

Tex entered the pool area through the pool house and moved to stand behind Wally in the lanai.

"Evening."

He kept his voice as neutral as possible, given the fact that he wanted to explode with laughter. The look on Charlotte's face was priceless.

"Wally, what are you still doing here, man? I thought you had class tonight. And what about that article you're supposed to be writing?"

"Just gathering more information, boss. Thought I might include a section on potbellied pigs, considering the research opportunity that your classes with Toto afford." Wally dragged his foot off the chair and glanced at his watch and then up at Charlotte. "I'll catch you later?"

"I...uh, okay." Wide-eyed, Charlotte sent a helpless glance at Tex.

Tex shrugged.

Wally began to trot backward toward the gate. "Bye, Charlotte."

"Goodbye, Wally."

Tex remained in possession of his poise until Wally had trudged to his car and disappeared down the driveway.

"Do you think I can learn to speak pig?" Charlotte wondered aloud, and Tex let go of the chunk of his inner cheek that he was biting and started to laugh.

He laughed the kind of contagious belly laugh that relieves tension and creates a camaraderie with the ones it infects. As he sank to the edge of Charlotte's lounge chair and howled at the ceiling of the lanai, she began to giggle. Soon, they were doubled over with thigh-slapping hilarity. Faces scrunched, tears sprang to their eyes and rolled down their cheeks.

"He was serious?" Charlotte wondered.

Tex could only nod.

Their gales of laughter turned the heads of the servants in the kitchen and caused knowing smiles. Tex dragged a hand over his face. His stomach hurt and his cheeks ached. He couldn't remember laughing this hard since he was a little kid. The fact that Charlotte sat there, wheezing and clutching his arm, only made him laugh harder.

Finally, the minutes of incapacitating laughter began to ebb into the occasional burst, and then into companionable guffaws and giggles.

Charlotte dabbed her eyes with the corner of her towel. "Where did you get this guy?"

With exaggeration, Tex stared at her. "Read my mind."

Charlotte pressed her temples, and closed her eyes. "I'm beginning to pick up signals."

For the first time since they met, they felt easy with

each other. Charlotte leaned back and pushed her sunglasses up on her head. Tex twisted in his seat to better face her and bridging her long, slender legs with his arm, leaned on the opposite side of the lounger. Her brightly painted toenails rested a hair's breadth from his wrist. Her feet were adorable. He longed to pull them into his lap and give them a little massage. Instead, he gathered his wits and answered her question.

"Actually, I inherited Wally. Payback for a practical joke I played on another clinic. Long story. Suffice it to say, Wally is several fries short of a Happy Meal, but his uncle funded the University's Veterinary Sciences wing, so there you go."

"Ahh." Charlotte shifted in her chair and her toes came to rest against his wrist. "What made you decide to become an animal behaviorist?"

Tex shrugged. "Natural progression, I guess. I've always been really good with dogs and horses. I don't know why. They just respond to me."

Her nod indicated interest, so, even though he'd made himself a promise about becoming too friendly with Charlotte, he continued. Against his better judgment.

"For about twenty years now, I've been breaking horses—"

"*Twenty* years?" Charlotte leaned forward and stared. "How old are you, anyway?"

"I'll be thirty on my next birthday."

"So you started breaking horses when you were ten?"

"Mm-hmm. Started hanging around the stables and pestering the ranch hands when I was nine or ten. Shocked everyone when I managed to gentle one savage beast that everyone had given up on as hopeless."

"Wow. Have you always loved animals?"

"Yep." He arched one brow. "Have you always hated them?"

"I told you, I don't *hate* them. I just don't see any reason to have them running all over the house."

"Did you ever have pets when you were a kid?"

"No." He detected a defensive note in her voice. "And I don't think that's so weird. I don't feel deprived."

Tex shrugged. "You don't miss what you never had."

"You make it sound like I didn't have a normal childhood, or something."

"Well, did you?"

"Yes. It's my adulthood that's been strange."

When Charlotte smiled, it was as if the setting sun pulled back off the horizon. "Tell me," he urged, suddenly wanting to know everything about her, from A to Z.

"No," she protested.

"Why not?"

"Because! We're talking about you. Finish telling me how you got into the animal behavior business."

"Oh, right." He inched forward, wanting to infringe on her space, just a little. His wrist leaned a little more heavily on her ankle. She didn't move away. "Well, like I said, I always had a knack with horses. The bigger and meaner they were, the better I liked 'em."

She shuddered. "You're brave."

"Nah. Just nuts."

"That, too."

"So anyway, people started bringing me their problem horses. Then, folks found out I was good at training cow dogs, and started asking me to train their dogs—"

"What's a cow dog?"

"You really are a city slicker, aren't you? It's part cow and part dog."

"You lie!"

Tex laughed. "It's a herd dog. Like a sheep dog. Only for cows."

"Okay, continue."

"Well, that led into training seeing-eye dogs, patrol and special task dogs for the police force, and then police horses, and then pet obedience courses for owners and that led to some advice on handling horses for film and television."

"Wow. How wonderful."

Tex could tell by the interest in her eyes, that she was serious. "I thought you'd think my line of work was a living hell."

"No. If you like your work, that's wonderful." She pushed at her cuticles with her thumbnail. "I'll be lucky to even have a job, let alone a job I like."

"Oh, yeah. I've been meaning to ask. How'd the job search go today?"

"It was dismal. Nobody I talked to needs someone with my job experience."

"What is your experience?"

"I took care of my nanna Dorothy for ten years after I graduated from high school. She passed away a month ago."

"I'm sorry."

"Don't be. I loved her and miss her very much. And in many ways, I was dependent on her. But I'm fine. She lived to be a hundred and she had a full life, the last ten years of which she had a personal attendant. Me." Charlotte sighed. "I'm an only child. My mom and dad married late in life and both died of natural causes while I was still in high school. So I was the only one left to care for Nanna."

"What kind of work are you looking for?"

"I don't know yet. Right now, I'd be willing to settle for anything that pays minimum wage. I need to start earning some money so her pig and I can eat."

"So, she left her pig to you."

"Yeah. Nanna Dorothy loved Toto like a baby. She was a bit of an eccentric. Anyway, in her will she demanded that I take over where she left off, and, uh, love Toto like a baby."

"How can she force you to do that?"

"By holding my inheritance up until Toto is dead of natural causes."

"Ouch. That could be years."

"Tell me about it. I need a job. Fast."

For a long, silent moment, they simply looked at each other, not moving, lest they break the spell. Their conversation was so candid and relaxed that it surprised them both.

Tex was completely mesmerized. He'd misjudged her. Charlotte wasn't the lazy debutante that he'd originally thought. Instead, she was caring, loving and courageous. All of the things he admired in a woman.

Warning bells sounded in the back of his mind.

He was beginning to let his emotions take over. The way he had with Jennifer. With Jennifer, he'd told himself that her allergy to his line of work didn't matter. That they could overcome that obstacle and be happy together.

But he'd been wrong.

And getting any more deeply involved with the beauty who reclined beneath his arm would be a mistake. Deliberately, he pulled his arm from where it was propped over her body and levered himself off the end of her lounge chair.

"Well," he said, feeling suddenly awkward and needing to get away. His mind was a muddle. He needed to think about what was happening to him, where Charlotte was concerned, and he couldn't do that with her lying there in that skimpy suit. "Sounds to me like you need a decent resume." Tex cleared his throat, and squinted into the sunset.

"That would no doubt help," she agreed.

"Probably better get on that, so that you can...you know...get on your own two feet." He backed out of the lanai. "I just remembered, I've got to be somewhere. I'll see you tomorrow."

Charlotte nodded, a bewildered expression tugging at her delicate features. "Uh, okay. Sure. Ten?"

"Yeah. Ten."

Before he could change his mind and crawl into that lounger with her and take her into his arms and kiss those pouty lips, Tex turned on his heel and stalked off.

Chapter Four

Four days had passed since their eye-opening conversation and Charlotte still had no idea why Tex had turned so distant. The winds of fate seemed to have changed at the end of their discussion in the lanai that day. Over and over, she dissected their visit, trying to discern the sudden change in his attitude toward her. It was so strange. There they'd been, having a perfectly nice talk and wham-o, the shutters came down behind his eyes.

Had she said something to offend him? If so, what?

Since then, they'd continued to work closely together with Toto, but there were none of the sparks that she'd been sure she felt during their first lesson. Progress with the pig was slow, too.

It didn't help matters that she'd been too busy to read the assigned material. He thought she was an educational slacker and an animal hater, and they'd gone back to bickering, as if their friendly interlude had never happened.

However, not everything was quite so bleak on the

social front. Wally had a midterm paper due that had kept him home typing for several days, and he'd been unable to pester her any further about his "rapid-progression" and "silent-communication" theories.

And Hunt had dropped by every day to flirt. Today he'd even invited her to a dance. A hoedown type affair, put on by Big Daddy twice a year, that Hunt claimed all the ranch hands attended. It had sounded like a pleasant diversion to Charlotte, so she'd agreed, though she secretly wished Tex had been the one to do the asking. In any event, Hunt seemed like a sweet guy. Certainly not as volatile as Tex. But not as sexy either.

She needed to get Tex out of her mind.

With a heavy sigh, Charlotte shifted her position on the lounge chair in the lanai, where she'd taken up residence these past days. Her attraction to this spot was twofold. On the one hand, she kept hoping Tex would happen by and they could pick up their conversation where they left off. And on the other hand, it was the one place she could rest and relax after a depressing day of searching for jobs. Jobs for which she was not qualified.

The newspaper crackled as she refolded the meager classified section of the *Hidden Valley Tribune Appeal*. Red pen in hand, she scanned the listings, hoping against hope that there would be something new in there. Something that she had not yet applied for. And been turned down for.

Nope. No. Nothing.

Rats.

Except...

Her eyes strayed to the bottom of the page, where a line of bold print caught her attention. This was not a local ad, but it was interesting.

AT-HOME MAKEUP COMPANY

Opportunity awaits!

Looking for a challenging career in the glamorous world of fashion? Work in the privacy of your own home and earn up to $100,000 a year in commission. The sky is the limit as you are your own boss! This national company is actively recruiting positive, outgoing, hardworking people to answer this exciting opportunity of a lifetime. No experience necessary, we train for free. Don't miss out!

Call 1-800-555-ATHM today!

$100,000 a year? Wow! Most of the jobs she'd been applying for in Hidden Valley offered only a dollar or two above minimum wage, with tips, even in the best case scenario. Excitement flooded her body, causing her to tingle all over. She was positive, outgoing, hardworking. And the best part? She had no experience!

She was perfect for this job.

Although she wasn't much for wearing a lot of makeup, she'd always been very creative with art supplies in school. Makeup couldn't be that much different.

Charlotte drew a red circle around the ad, then slipped her toes into her sandals and grabbed her bathing suit cover-up. She could hardly wait to get into the house and call this number. If she didn't hurry, she might be left out. Surely everyone who saw this ad would be rushing to jam the phone lines.

Yep. A buoyant smile tugged Charlotte's lips. If corporate America didn't want her, she'd simply have to create her own position. If there was one thing Charlotte took pride in, it was her ability to be flexible.

She'd find her hidden talent. It was simply a matter of time.

* * *

"I can't stay long today, I have to work." Charlotte said, taking a seat in one of the comfortable club chairs that sat before Tex's desk.

"That's okay." Tex shrugged in an attempt to hide his disappointment.

What she did on her own time was her business, although he couldn't help but be curious about the new job she'd started just two days ago. The sad truth was, Tex couldn't help but be curious about everything that concerned Charlotte Beauchamp. That was the problem.

He avoided eye contact with her and shuffled some paperwork as she set her coffee cup on his desk, stirred in generous helpings of cream and sugar and then gave the edge of her cup a couple of taps with her spoon. He was beginning to memorize her routines.

Bad sign.

Every morning at ten, just before they got started, they would meet—as he did with all of his clients—and discuss the prior day's training progress. The conversations with Charlotte were brief and that was fine with Tex. It was hard enough sitting so close to her. Working with her for a solid hour every day. Watching her sit back and cross her shapely legs, toss her thick, curly hair out of her eyes, bring the coffee mug to her full lips.

Keeping his distance was becoming a real chore.

By the way she bickered with him lately, Tex could tell he'd hurt her feelings last week in the lanai, by leaving in such an abrupt manner. But it couldn't be helped. He had to keep his distance from her, and this was the only way he knew how. In the long run, it was better for them both.

Before thinking through the prudence of striking up a conversation with her, he heard himself blurt out, "So. You got a job."

"Yes."

He hated himself for probing, but he was dying of curiosity. "Where?"

"I don't really have an office, per se. It's a job in sales."

"Sales? What kind of sales?"

"I'm an account executive for the At-Home Makeup Company," she informed him. The note of pride in her voice was unmistakable.

"Well, congratulations."

"Thank you. I'm having my first party tonight, and I want to make sure everything is ready."

"Party?"

"We sell our products at in-home parties."

Tex frowned. What had she gotten herself into? Charlotte was a real babe in the woods, when it came to the job world. Some primal protective streak forced him to probe further. "You're going to make a living by throwing parties?"

Charlotte bristled and he could tell that perhaps his choice of words had struck a raw nerve. "What's wrong with that? It's perfectly legal, it's fun, it's interesting and best of all, profitable. You can make up to a hundred thousand dollars a year, if you're willing to work hard."

Tex snorted. "Have to party pretty hardy and sell a helluva lot of lipstick to make a hundred grand."

Setting her coffee cup on his desk, Charlotte crossed her arms in a defensive posture across her chest. "Well, I probably won't make that much my first year, but eventually—after I take the required cosmetology correspondence courses—I hope to go for my diamond tiara."

The feisty look that sparked in her eyes made his blood pound in his ears. Man, she was cute when she got all fired up about something. Which was most of the time.

He hated to burst her bubble, but seemed to him that this whole thing sounded too good to be true. He raised a skeptical brow. "Diamond...tiara?"

"Yes," she snapped, jaw jutting. "There are different levels of achievement in a career with At-Home. First, it's a crystal perfume bottle. Then a silver mascara wand, then a sapphire-and-ruby lipstick case and then, when you are making top dollars, the diamond tiara. That's my goal."

"Sounds like you've got it all figured out."

"Look. I can tell by your tone of voice that you think this is all just a bunch of hooey. But you're wrong. You just wait and see."

"I believe you."

"No you don't, but that's okay." With a deep breath, she sat up, ramrod straight and eyed him through long-lashed slits. "Mock me if you will. But tonight I'm going to surprise you. Miss Clarise is acting as my hostess. We are inviting all the ladies in the neighborhood and as many of her relatives as we could think of. I believe some of your sisters may even drive down from college tonight."

"Which ones?"

"The ones named after states."

Tex chuckled. "Everyone in our family is named after states of the union."

For a moment, she dropped her defensive posture. "Really?"

"Yep." He leaned back in his chair and recounted for her. "There's Dakota, Montana, me, and Kentucky, who goes by Tucker. There are five girls. Virginia, who everyone calls Ginny, then there is Carolina, Georgia, Maryland who is Mary for short, and last but not least little

Louise-Anna. We call her Lucy, unless she's in trouble, which is often. She's still in high school."

"Wow." Charlotte's eye's were open wide. "I bet they all wear makeup," she mused.

"Not the guys."

For the first time in a week, Charlotte smiled at him. Completely dazzled, Tex basked in this glow until he realized he was staring like some kind of lovesick teen. He pushed his chair away from his desk and reverted behind the safety zone of his cool facade.

"We'd probably better quit wasting time and get to work." He knew his tone was more clipped than strictly necessary, but he was speaking more to himself than to her. As he strode to the door, he only hoped that the Texas sun was cooler than his face.

This was not going well at all.

Charlotte's heart was pounding at the speed of light and it felt as if she should have washed her hands in antiperspirant, so damp were her palms. One day of rehearsal and product study was clearly not enough. She felt light-headed and it sounded as if electrical power lines were buzzing in her ears.

Didn't matter. She'd muddle through. She had to. Miss Clarise had nearly sixty ladies, most of whom Charlotte had never laid eyes on in her life, seated in her parlor, nibbling on fancy party fare as Charlotte fumbled to set up her easel, flip charts, color wheels and multitude of confusing makeup supply cases.

Show time.

After she'd introduced herself and given her rather unpolished spiel on the history and credo of the At-Home Makeup Company, the room full of women sat in silent anticipation, waiting for Charlotte to begin her makeover demonstration on EttaMae Hanson who was seated on a stool in the center of the room.

EttaMae was Big Daddy's pastry chef and Fuzzy the ranch hand's sweetheart.

Frumpy, lumpy and grumpy, EttaMae had seemed like the perfect candidate for transformation with the miraculous At-Home Makeup products, back when Charlotte was in the planning stages. Back when she was all alone and didn't have a room full of women hanging on her every word. Back when she was organized and could find her notes.

Charlotte wiped her damp palms on her slacks and tried to muster a confident smile. She could do this. She wouldn't let a little stage fright hold her back.

She'd practiced all afternoon on the dummy that had come with her supplies, but the trouble was, EttaMae looked nothing like the perfectly proportioned dummy.

"Okay. Uh. EttaMae has what we call, uh," she squinted and groped for something professional to say as she tentatively probed EttaMae's face with her fingertips, "combination skin." Whatever that was.

EttaMae grunted.

A stretchy headband had gathered the older woman's hair into a graying haystack at the top of her large head. In fact, so large was her head, that it now appeared to be roughly the size of New Hampshire. Gracious, EttaMae was all face. This would take an eternity.

"This means that we will use our all purpose base to smooth out those imperfections and give EttaMae a...er, healthy glow."

Again, EttaMae grunted.

Ladies shifted in their seats to better see. Order forms rustled in their laps. One woman coughed. All five of Tex's lovely sisters sat together on one couch whispering among themselves and scanning the literature she'd provided.

Charlotte's nerves were more tightly strung than piano strings.

I can do this, I can. I think I can. I think I can. Charlotte held her color palette up next to EttaMae's ruddy, mottled cheek. "First," she sang, quoting the literature, "we will color match and then we will test patch."

And turn, two, three. And smile, two, three. And nod, two, three with carefree confidence at the audience. "Our special formulas," she ad-libbed, "are blended in secret laboratories to be gentle to even the sensitive skin of a newborn's behind."

EttaMae frowned and grunted.

"Now, to select the proper season in order to, uh... um...best figure out...uh, what color she is. Okay. EttaMae looks to be a...uh...spring. No...um...summer... hmm, that's not right..." Charlotte studied the season color palette, and then the older woman. EttaMae looked more like seasoned shoe leather. "No...I think, fall. So we'll try one of our autumn colors for the hearty complexion on her first. I think SouthWest Sunset will be just about right."

"Sounds romantic," Miss Clarise put in helpfully.

Her friends murmured in polite agreement.

Charlotte dabbed a blob of color on EttaMae's cheek and rubbed it in. "Okay, the match looks good. While we give the test patch a moment, I'd just like to turn your attention to the information on the back of your forms about a potential career with the At-Home Makeup Company. If any of you are interested, it is possible to earn up to a hundred thousand dollars a year in commission, working only a few days a week, in the comfort of your own home."

Ladies, dripping with diamonds and designer clothing trimmed in fur sat motionless. Apparently they did not need the money, Charlotte thought, her cheeks growing warm. Well, this was a special crowd. Not all of her parties would be for women this affluent.

She glanced at EttaMae.

The skin beneath the SouthWest Sunset primer coat seemed to be turning a lovely shade of…fiery SouthWest sunset. Charlotte grabbed a tissue and scrubbed the makeup off. "That's odd," she murmured.

"Is it supposed to burn like that?" EttaMae groused.

Everyone leaned forward to get a better look. Women frowned and began to confab amongst themselves. Miss Clarise summoned an ice pack and Charlotte had EttaMae hold it to the angry-looking welt on the side of her face.

"It feels like I've been slapped," EttaMae complained.

"Our products can be a bit bracing to those with sensitive skin."

EttaMae gingerly touched her cheek. "More like abusive."

"I…uh…" Charlotte beamed at the audience. "Did I mention our fantastic selection of lipsticks?"

As she dug around in one of her cases she heard a commotion from the couch where Tex's sisters were seated. Glancing up, she noticed them waving at someone out in the hall, beyond the pillared arches.

Tex.

From where she stood, she could see his broad grin.

What on earth was *he* doing here? Charlotte's pulse became thready and she shot him a "go home" look.

He ignored it.

"I'd like EttaMae to try our Plumberry Wine Everlasting Lipcolor," Charlotte announced and, forcing her attention back to the job at hand, smeared a slash of color across EttaMae's thin lips. "The special dyes in these products are semipermanent for color that won't rub off."

"Se-ni-*pen-an-ant?*" EttaMae gasped from between her suddenly swelling lips. "I don wan ny lits ta de dis color *ferebber!*"

"No, no, no," Charlotte's nervous laughter rang out. "The color should only last for one day." She peered at EttaMae's lips which were now as furious as her cheek. "EttaMae, do you suffer from allergies?"

"No!"

"Not to anything?"

"No!"

"I don't understand," Charlotte murmured. To the crowd, she said, "Not to worry, ladies. I have everything under control. EttaMae will be fine." Again, nervous laughter bubbled up and past her lips. "No one has ever died from using At-Home products." *I hope,* she added silently.

"Died?" EttaMae shrieked.

Tex took a step into the room and hovered near Miss Clarise under the archway. His smile had changed from skeptical to reassuring and for that Charlotte would be forever grateful as the women in the audience all exchanged glances of alarm. Some twittered and the murmurings became more audible. Several made wisecracks about getting 911 on their cell phones and there was laughter.

Well, at least on one level, people were enjoying themselves, Charlotte thought, feeling the hysteria rise. Miss Clarise had another ice pack delivered by one of the staff, and Charlotte held it to EttaMae's lips.

"No, no, no," Charlotte said with a confidence she was nowhere near feeling. "EttaMae, don't worry. Watch. I'll try some of the lip color myself."

With her free hand, Charlotte reached for a lipstick and peering into the cheval mirror that Miss Clarise had loaned her for the party, applied a generous coat.

Hmm.

Charlotte frowned.

Felt like a million tiny needles were poking holes in her lips.

"Doth id peel wike tins and needles are tingling your lits?" she asked EttaMae.

"Yeth." EttaMae pushed the ice bag away to reveal her ballooning lips. "I think thombody thould tall the dotor!"

"Tall the dotor?" Charlotte repeated. "Yeth, thath's a good itea."

Ever gracious, Miss Clarise stepped to Charlotte's side and announced that there would be an intermission in the program and asked if the ladies would be so good as to follow her to the dining room for refreshments and a live classical music interlude.

Clearly enjoying themselves, the women—all chattering like magpies—followed Miss Clarise out of the room. EttaMae pulled off her plastic cape and headed to the powder room to inspect the damage.

Alone and feeling embarrassed, Charlotte slogged over to the couch where Tex's sisters had been sitting and sank into its buttery depths. Tears sprang into her eyes and she buried her head in her hands. Finding her way in this world was going to be a little harder than she'd thought.

Still standing in the doorway, Tex hovered uncertainly. She cut such a lonely figure, sitting there, shoulders slumped, head bowed. His heart lurched at the sight. He'd never been good with tears. Didn't matter who was crying, he'd always felt the need to make the tears stop.

Although he had the suspicion that there was a little more to it than that, where Charlotte was concerned. His need to protect her was beyond the shirttail relative phase.

He glanced down at Toto, who'd been sitting comfortably on his boot. "Come on, pig," he murmured.

Knowing he was probably making a monumental mistake by allowing himself to follow his instincts, he moved over to where she sat and settling in next to her, took her hand.

Toto trotted after him.

Seeming to sense that something was not quite right on the emotional front, the little pig laid his snout down on the seat of the couch, between Tex and Charlotte's knees, and blinked up at them as if he understood that something was amiss. He breathed heavily, but did not move.

"Hey," Tex whispered, and ran a finger down her cheeks. Her lips were puffy and plum-colored and he fought the urge to find out if they tasted as delectable as they looked.

Charlotte sniffed and smiled. Tiny lines forked at the corners of her watery eyes. "Hi."

"How you doin'?"

She batted at her melancholia with her free hand. "I'll de otay." A heavy sigh escaped her lips. "It's dust gooen to de a natter o' tinding what I'n thuited to do. There'th a career out there tor ne, I dust know it."

"I hope so," Tex muttered.

"It dothn't help that you are tho anxiouths to get rid o' ne," she snapped.

"No, no, that's not what I…" Tex tipped her chin up with his thumb and looked deep into her eyes. "I'm sorry."

She sniffed.

"Does it hurt?"

"Only when I thmile."

"Would it help if I kissed it better?" He was teasing her, trying to lighten the mood, but there was a serious question underlying the play.

"I...I don't know..."

She peeked at him from beneath the fringe of her lashes, and for an instant Tex thought he could see mirrored there the attraction he felt. Without stopping to analyze the sanity of his actions, he slipped an arm around her shoulders and gathered her into his embrace. She came to him, without protest, as he had feared she might.

Lightly, she rested a palm over the staccato beat of his heart and he wondered if she could feel the effect she was having. Their gazes locked and held, and for the longest moment, the feelings that they'd been battling rushed to the forefront, and became evident in their expressions of longing.

Ever so slowly, Tex lowered his mouth to hers in a kiss so gossamer, so incredibly sweet, he found it hard to believe that an experience this exquisite could be of this earth. He wanted to be gentle, knowing that her mouth was tender. But he was driven to deepen the kiss. Angling her mouth more firmly beneath his, he kissed her the way he'd dreamed of kissing Charlotte Beauchamp since the very moment he'd laid eyes on her; with every ounce of fire and passion that made up their love/hate relationship. Her lips were soft and sweet and she tasted of mint and Plumberry Wine Everlasting Color and a feminine essence that was uniquely Charlotte.

He could feel her lungs laboring together with his as their breathing became ragged. Hands searching, he pushed the silken masses of her glorious hair away from her face and traced the delicate contours of her cheek-bones with his fingertips.

"Mmm." Never had Tex's heart worked so hard. His head felt dizzy and his eyes went dark and blurry. Little pinspots of light danced before him, and it was almost as if he'd left his body and was enjoying this experience on another level altogether.

He let his fingertips wander from her cheeks to her jaw, and then tentatively to her lips. The air stirred between them as he whispered against her mouth. "All better?"

"No." Charlotte groaned and her eyes slid shut. "My lipths thar dead," she moaned.

Tex sat back. "Then you couldn't feel any of that?"

She gave her head a sad shake and Tex didn't know whether to laugh or cry. Feeling suddenly foolish, he realized that he'd put everything he had into that kiss.

His body was alert, in tune with her every move. Every nerve ending that made up his entire being—including his suddenly tingling lips—was supercharged with awareness of Charlotte.

And she hadn't felt a thing.

"Oh well," he sighed, struggling for his composure. Struggling to salvage the situation. "I'm sure it will wear off eventually. Maybe we can try again then," he teased, hope tingeing his voice.

Again, Charlotte moaned, and he wasn't quite sure how to take this response.

Was this a moan of dread?

Ecstasy?

Tex slipped his hands from her face to his and palming his cheeks, rubbed his eyes and brows with his fingers. It was beginning to look like kissing her had been a mistake. What the heck had he been thinking? She wasn't looking for a relationship with him. She was looking for a sympathetic shoulder to cry on. Nothing more. Nothing less.

With an ability born of much practice since Jennifer, Tex erected the walls back up around his heart, even as Charlotte lay against him, her arms coiled about his neck, and her tears dampening the fabric of his shirt.

Footfalls clicked on the mahogany behind them and Miss Clarise's soft gasp met them as she stepped into the room. "Oh!" Bright blue eyes sparkling, Miss Clarise took a step back. "Forgive me. I didn't mean to intrude."

Self-consciously, Charlotte sprang away from Tex's embrace and tried to feign normalcy. "Thath's otay."

Tex straightened his shirt. "You're not intruding."

"Oh." Miss Clarise soft chuckle was knowing. "Well, in any event, I won't keep you."

Smile watery, Charlotte stood. "Thankth to Texth, I'm fine, Mith Clarith. I thould be ready to dit dack to work now."

"Well, that's something I needed to talk to you about, Charlotte dear. It would seem that many of the ladies must be on their way. Everyone thanks you for a truly wonderful, entertaining time and they are taking their literature home with them, for further product study. Tex, your sisters say to tell you goodbye, and Charlotte, they'll all call you about an order, in the morning."

"Thath's all right, Mith Clarith. I'm retiring form thith bithineth. Tell dem not to theel obligated to thpend any noney."

"All right, dear." Miss Clarise nodded. "Big Daddy and I will see the ladies out, so you just relax, darlin'. Sit for a while. We can have the maids clean up your supplies and deliver them to your suite later. Then perhaps we'll call the doctor and have him come take a look at you and EttaMae.''

"Otay."

Feeling like an overcooked strand of spaghetti, Charlotte puddled back to the couch. Balefully, she stared first at Miss Clarise as the tiny matriarch retreated to bid adieu to her guests, and then at Tex, whose expression was so caring and sweet, it made her want to weep all over again. "The ladieth are leafing. After only thirty minuths."

Tex nodded. "But it's not your fault."

"Yeth. Yeth it ith."

Quivering, sniffing, seemingly wanting to console, Toto prodded her knee with his snout and made little sympathetic grunts in his throat. Charlotte pushed him away, but this did not daunt Toto. More aggressively now, he nudged her hand. When she did not respond, he moved between her legs and—standing between the couch and the coffee table—laid his head in her lap. Absently, Charlotte stroked his bristly head, and scratched that spot between his ears that he seemed to enjoy so much.

Little grunts of pleasure crowded into his throat.

Tex leaned back on the couch and watched, his expression faraway. Pensive.

She wondered what he was thinking. Probably that she was the world's worst kisser. But hey, that wasn't her fault. He'd simply caught her on a bad day. She would make it up to him. He'd offered her another chance, and she was going to take it. Kissing Tex was not something she wanted to miss out on.

Gingerly, she reached up and touched the two pork chops that had become her lips. How mortifying.

And yet, Tex had kissed her. Consoled her. He was

such a neat man, when he wasn't being a condescending pain in the neck. For a moment she pondered the amazing truth that no woman had snapped this guy up yet and led him down to the altar.

Not that she was looking for a trip down the aisle. No. Charlotte had just escaped from the virtual prison of Nanna Dorothy's needs. Now, Charlotte wanted to strike out on her own. Forming a relationship with a man would certainly not further this cause.

Chapter Five

Lazy particles of dust floated in the sunlight that streamed through the veranda doors of Charlotte's suite. The golden haze flirted with her eyelids and urged her to wakefulness. From outside, birdsong serenaded. *Begin the day,* came the coaxing melody.

Charlotte didn't want to wake up. She was safe, and comfortable and warm. And, she'd been dreaming such a delicious, languid dream. Tex had been kissing her and ohhh…if those birds would just be quiet, she could go back to her dream world again. The lilting birdsong turned vicious, as the birds squabbled over territory under the eaves.

Charlotte sighed. Story of her life.

Slowly, her eyes opened and she glanced around the tastefully decorated suite that had once belonged to Big Daddy and Miss Clarise's daughter, Patsy, before she was married. The smell of rich, aromatic coffee filtered into her bedroom, tickling her senses. The maid had been here to deliver her breakfast, most likely because she hadn't made her usual trek to the dining room to eat with Big Daddy and Miss Clarise.

She glanced at the clock.

Nine-thirty?

Good heavens!

Hair tangled and filled with static cling, Charlotte bolted upright and peered in the giant, gilt-framed mirror that was situated on the wall above the dresser opposite the bed.

She'd overslept! No doubt because she spent half the night tossing and turning and reliving the horror of her ignominious entrance into the world of business.

That, and Tex's tender kiss.

She looked like something wild and furry the cat had slain, but at least her lips were back to normal. The salve that the doctor left for her and EttaMae had worked wonders, taking away the savage pain and helping to lessen the swelling.

The kindly doctor said that this was not his first At-Home Makeup house call, and that as far as he knew, the company'd had many complaints filed against it with the Better Business Bureau. Apparently, the company made its money by selling starter kits to well-meaning, unsuspecting women who longed to work from the home.

That was her, all right, Charlotte thought as she pulled her pajamas off over her head and headed to the bathroom for a quick shower, *a real rube.*

Fresh off the turnip truck.

Well, at least she'd learned a valuable lesson. Next time, she wouldn't be so trusting. Next time, she'd check out the history of the company, before she sent them any more of her precious money.

When she'd finished her shower, she dried and styled

her hair, then donned a sundress and slipped her feet into a pair of strappy sandals.

From the tray that the maids had left on her parlor area table, Charlotte grabbed two croissants—one for herself and one for the pig who'd somehow ended up sleeping at the foot of her bed last night—and the *Hidden Valley Tribune Appeal* classifieds section. With a quick glance, she scanned the listings. Jobs in Hidden Valley were hard to come by. Her gaze fell to the bold print at the bottom of the page where there was yet another very interesting national ad.

It seemed that the Action-Adventure Clothiers Company needed sharp sales people. Sounded right up her alley. She loved clothes. If she was ever going to get out there on her own, she needed to get back on the horse that threw her.

Sitting around feeling sorry for herself had never been Charlotte's style, because, if there was one thing that she prided herself on, it was that she had moxie. Pluck. A stubborn streak as broad as Toto's hindquarters. She'd find a job that suited her. It was simply a matter of time.

With one last check in the mirror to inspect her still Plumberry Wine-colored lips, Charlotte called to Toto, and tossed him a bit of bread.

"Ready for class?"

Toto grunted.

"Yeah. Me neither. I feel really embarrassed about last night."

Toto stared up at her, through his tiny, poorly sighted eyes. He smacked his lips and nudged her hand, so she broke off another piece of croissant and fed it to him.

"I know, you were there. Was it all really as awful as I remember?"

Head swaying, Toto maintained eye contact and, lowering himself to his haunches, allowed his pink-and-black spotted belly to rest upon his rear hooves.

"No?" Charlotte cocked her head and regarded her pig as she thoughtfully nibbled her croissant. "You're trying to tell me you enjoyed yourself? That's sweet of you to say." She sighed and gave her head a sharp shake. "I can't believe I'm talking to a pig. Maybe Wally was right," she muttered.

She couldn't help noticing that Toto's eyes never left hers.

"Weird."

Toto squealed.

"No, not you. Anyway, thanks for your support, pig." She dragged her gaze from Toto's and peeked once more into the mirror. Lightly, she ran her fingers across her lower lip, wondering, wanting to know, what the feel of Tex's lips on hers was really like. "You know, Toto, the best part of the whole night was getting a kiss out of the deal. Too bad I couldn't feel a thing."

Charlotte's mind flashed back, as it had been doing all night, to the moment Tex took her into his arms and settled his mouth over hers, and her body tightened. Even with numb lips, it had been one of life's sweetest moments. A memory she would treasure forever.

She glanced at the clock. Almost ten. Her heart palpitated.

Why was she so nervous about this morning's lesson? They'd had dozens already.

Perhaps it was because their evening had ended so awkwardly, last night. Tex had walked her to her door. The doctor's balm had already begun to work, and she was looking forward to another opportunity to kiss Tex. To kiss him back, anyway. She'd waited for him to make the move, but he'd given her a brotherly hug, then disappeared down the hall.

Their original kiss must have been pretty bad.

And now, she had to face him again.

She'd play it cool. Obviously, that's how he wanted it, if his brotherly hug was any indication, he wasn't up for another lifeless kiss. Her face flamed.

"Come on, pig," she called and together they trotted down the massive marble staircase and into the bright morning sunshine.

It was as awkward as he'd feared.

Tex watched Charlotte absently pour far too much cream and sugar into her coffee. She was acting just a tad too bright. A tad too perky. As if what had passed between them last night was a mere aberration.

He knew he never should have kissed her. They were obviously all wrong for each other.

"I brought the help wanted ads with me today."

"Oh?"

"Yes, I found something in here that looks interesting. If it's all right with you, I'd like to call the Better Business Bureau to check up on them, before I get started."

"Good idea." The springs in his chair creaked as he settled back in his seat to regard her. "What kind of company is it?"

"Clothing. Fashion."

"What's the name?"

"Action-Adventure Clothiers."

"Never heard of them."

"They're not local."

His heart clutched and he struggled to remain nonchalant. "Does this mean you'll be moving?"

"I'm working on that," she snapped.

This time, she'd taken his question the wrong way. "No," he hastened to reassure her, "I just wondered if you would have an office in town, or somewhere else." Somewhere too far from here.

"No, this is another company that throws the 'at home' parties."

He quirked a brow.

"Tex, not all companies that work out of the home are scams. Tupperware, case in point. Hugely successful."

"Then why don't you sell Tupperware?"

"I might." She tapped the paper with her finger. "But first I want to give this a go. I love clothes. I think this could be my calling."

"Well, good luck."

"Thanks."

From the other side of the room, there was a thumping and scratching noise. Charlotte stiffened and looked at Tex with wide eyes. "What was that?"

Tex gestured to the plastic dog carrier in the corner. "Kitty must be waking up."

"Kitty?"

He went to retrieve the carrier. "You want to meet Kitty?"

"Do I have any choice?"

The door swung open at Tex's prodding and he reached inside for a bundle of what looked like sheep's wool.

Charlotte squinted. "Unless I really am species challenged, that is no cat."

"You're right. This little girl is a golden retriever puppy. I volunteer from time to time to be a puppy raiser for a friend of mine who runs a guide dog school in Dallas. Kitty here is only eight weeks now. After she spends a year following me everywhere, she'll be ready for instruction at the school in Dallas. Then she'll be placed with a blind, or visually impaired person.''

"Why don't you train her?''

"I could. I have. I'm licensed. But right now, my business is growing so fast, I don't have the time. I will again someday, though.'' He held the fluff-ball toward her. "Want to hold her?''

"Uh, no thank you.''

"Ah, come on. Do me a favor. Hold her while I go get her puppy food.''

He dumped the yawning round ball of fur into her lap and disappeared. Toto trotted forward to inspect this new addition to the animal farm.

Clumsily, Charlotte cradled the mutt, who gazed at her through sleepy eyes. "Kitty, huh? Where'd you get such a silly name?''

The puppy yawned. "Mmm.'' Charlotte smiled. "You're so sweet.'' She brought the pup up to her nose for a better view, when the dog latched on and began to nurse. Charlotte giggled. "You goosey thing. Give me my nose back.''

She pulled the puppy back into her lap and sat her down, the way she would seat a child. Fat paws flopping over her wrist, Kitty—round, pink belly irresistible to the touch—sat in contentment and gazed around the room.

"Don't tell Tex I said this, cuz, I'd deny it, but you are pretty cute. Yes. You are. Isn't this girl cute, Toto?'' At the sound of his name, Toto poked his nose into her lap and gave the pup another curious once-over with his snout. "Don't get any ideas, though,'' she warned the pig. "You are an only child, and it's going to stay that way.''

Tex watched for several minutes from the storeroom through the crack in the door as Charlotte cuddled the pup. His grin spread all the way to his gut. Charlotte Beauchamp, ice maiden when it came to animals, was beginning to thaw.

Oh, she liked to put on a frosty facade, but inside, she was as squishy as a warm Twinkie. Anybody who'd lay a puppy across their face and loudly smooch its belly, and then coo a bunch of feminine gobbledy-goop into its floppy ears was becoming a dog lover. Whether she was aware of it or not.

It hadn't escaped his notice either, that lately she'd softened considerably where Toto was concerned. Oh, she wasn't exactly kissing and cooing over him, but they'd become quite amicable. Even friendly with each other.

Perhaps there was hope for her after all, he mused.

Tex pushed through the door to his office and hefted the fifty-pound bag of puppy food up on a shelf that was already loaded with food for older dogs. Deciding not to draw attention to the fact that Charlotte was having a regular conversation with the animals, he nodded out the window and indicated the activity in the paddock.

"Looks like Big Daddy is getting ready for the hoe-down he's throwing tonight."

In the time since he and Charlotte had been visiting that morning, a party equipment rental company had arrived. An army of men were unloading trucks that had parked in the grassy area next to the classic red barn on the other side of the stables. Huge white tents were being set up, and beneath those, the barbecue area and an endless expanse of buffet tables.

Taking the puppy with her, Charlotte moved to stand beside Tex and watch the bustling activity going on outside.

A parquet dance floor had been hauled up to the hay mow and assembled. Dining tables and chairs followed. A van pulled up and a group of men disembarked and began unloading instruments and sound equipment into the barn. Twinkly lights were being strung to outline the barn and over the bushes and around fences. Searchlights were being positioned at the barn's entrance.

As usual, Big Daddy was going all out.

"Should be fun," Charlotte said. She looked up from Kitty and smiled.

"Yeah." He met her gaze and decided that there was no one more alluring than Charlotte when she smiled. He swallowed, and wondered if she might consider going to the dance with him. "I'm going to be there," he tossed out in his most offhand manner, fishing. Hoping.

"Me, too. Hunt asked me."

His heart stalled and went into a free fall. "Oh." Well, that answered that. She was going with Hunt. He'd waited too long. "Then I guess I'll be seeing you there."

Back out the window, her gaze shifted, still too bright. A tad too perky. "Sure."

"Come on, pig," he called and went out into the training yard, kicking himself the entire way.

As it was with all the parties Big Daddy threw—and he was well known for his lavish soirees—that evening's hoedown was a roaring success. Cars were parked all the way down both sides of the mile-long drive, and the field behind the stables resembled a city parking lot. The searchlights cut swaths of Hollywood into the darkening sky and attendants directed folks to the tents for drinks and assorted barbecued appetizers, and then on to the barn.

Charlotte entered the massive hay mow on Hunt's arm

with Toto hovering at her heels. They lingered near the doorway, orienting themselves and allowing their eyes to adjust to the dimmer light. Already the proceedings were in full swing.

Square dancers were being put through their paces by an ancient man who, though he looked fragile, could belt out the steps with the best of them. Knee pumping, he stomped his foot and clapped his hands and struggled to remain upright. With great gusto, the equally elderly band of old-timers sawed on their instruments and the joyful noise reverberated from the rafters to the floor and back again.

Indirect lighting illuminated bales of hay and balloons and streamers festooned antique ranch equipment. The walls were projected with colored light images of long horned cattle and cowboys on bucking broncos. Dry ice, like a London fog, spilled out of hidden machines and rolled and swirled across the floor.

It was truly a magical world.

Except for one thing.

Charlotte had yet to spot Tex.

Emotions warred within her. On the one hand, she was relieved not to have to bear the scrutiny of his probing gaze, as she had all morning. On the other hand, she had looked forward to the scrutiny of his probing gaze. Had styled her hair and carefully chosen her dress, specifically with his probing gaze in mind.

Her eyes darted about, searching the shadows for his familiar features, to no avail. Even as her heart sank, she clutched at the hope that Tex was simply late, and would arrive shortly.

Miss Clarise waved to her from across the room, and it was then Charlotte noticed that many of the neighbors who'd attended her makeup party were there. They, too, nodded and waved in a most cordial fashion and Charlotte pushed her mouth up at the corners and hoped she didn't look as foolish as she felt. They didn't seem to be laughing at her, so that much was good. Especially considering they'd probably be invited to another one of her sales parties in the not too distant future. She waved and feigned disappointment when Hunt urged her in the opposite direction, and over to the punch bowl.

Covertly, she continued to look for Tex.

Four of his sisters, Ginny, Mary, Carolina and Georgia were there with dates, some mingling, some dancing. They all called to Charlotte and beckoned her to join the fun. Even Wally was there, his eyes telegraphing silent, seductive messages from across the room.

Unfortunately, Tex was not with his intern. Not that she blamed him, of course. She took a deep breath and attempted to blow away her melancholy. Tex had said he was coming, she reminded herself. He would be there.

With a glance at Hunt and a shrug of her shoulders, Charlotte allowed herself to be swept to the dance floor and led through a series of complex dance moves that had her head swimming.

Never leaving Charlotte's side, Toto trotted after her on the dance floor, drawing the amused glances of the dancers who were forced to sidestep the little pig as he weaved in and out, do-se-do-ing and allemande lefting with the best of them. Just for the evening, she'd tied a red bandanna around his neck and strapped a straw hat to his head. His ears poked out through holes in the top and everyone agreed he looked quite jaunty.

"Come on, pig," Charlotte would call, when he'd get confused. Toto—corkscrew tail bobbing, hooves scrambling—would eventually catch up. Then, she would reward him with a bit of carrot she'd tucked into the pocket of her flouncy red gingham skirt.

Yes, Toto was the belle of the ball.

And, the food was fabulous. The music marvelous. The atmosphere, awesome. And, Hunt was a handsome, attentive date, bringing her punch and keeping the conversational ball rolling.

But, there was something elemental missing for Charlotte that evening, and she suspected even Hunt knew it was Tex.

Tex stood on the first landing of the stairs that led to the hay mow and listened to the party that was now in full swing. The floorboards overhead were vibrating with the feet that stomped to the lively beat of the music. He lifted his hat and rubbed his forehead with the back of his wrist.

The last place he wanted to be right now, was here. This whole thing would be torture, what with Charlotte and Hunt on a date and all. He contemplated turning around and heading home, but he'd promised Big Daddy and Miss Clarise that he'd attend.

Even so, they'd probably understand if he bailed.

Just before he pushed off the railing to leave, a porcine squeal from the top of the stairs caught his attention. Tex glanced up to spot Toto dancing from foot to foot, wriggling with delight at having spotted him.

Busted.

Charlotte was scrambling after the pig, her face flushed, her hair falling loose from her upswept hairdo. To Tex, she'd never looked more beautiful.

"Toto!" It was as she grabbed hold of his bandanna that she noticed Tex halfway down the stairs, and froze. "Hi."

The exertion had her breathing hard.

"Hi."

"I was beginning to think you weren't coming."

"So was I."

"Oh." She tugged the failing clip from her hair and raked the long masses of curls out of her eyes and over her shoulders. "Are you staying?"

"For a little while."

"Great. I mean, that's nice. Well, I'm…we're," she gestured to Toto, "in the middle of a dance with Hunt. But I expect I'll see you around…?"

"Don't keep him waiting on my account."

"Oh. Right."

Charlotte moved away and the throng on the dance floor swallowed her and Toto, too.

Since it was too late to back out now, Tex ambled up the steps and mingled with his aunt and sisters for a while, and then some of the ranch hands, his cousins, and some of the neighbors, but his gaze never strayed far from Charlotte.

Every now and again, he'd catch a glimpse of those endless legs, as that red, checkered skirt and those yards of starchy petticoats flew into the air. Boy, howdy, she was a doll, all sparkly-eyed and dewy-lipped, with her head tossed back, laughing at something amusing Hunt must have said.

She and Hunt seemed to be having a grand old time. Tex fished in his pocket for a stick of gum to keep from grinding his molars to bloody stumps. Oh, yeah. This was a barrel of monkeys.

After he'd been there awhile, Wally loped up to his side and settled next to him on a hay bale.

"Hey, boss."

"Hey, Wally." Ahh. This party just got better and better.

Wally nodded in Charlotte's direction. "If your cousin would ever stop dancing with that guy, I'd ask her to dance."

Yep. A veritable laugh riot. "She's not my cousin."

"Whatever."

"Well, Wally, old boy, if you can lure her away from her boyfriend, I'm sure she'd be obliged to dance with you." Obliged, being the operative word.

"Boyfriend?" Wally looked crestfallen. For a second. But only a second.

A little snowball of a gal, nearly swallowed in ruffles flounced by, capturing Wally's attention. "Watch this," he said to Tex, and focused his deep stare upon the woman.

As if she could feel the weight of his heavy gaze, the woman turned and smiled. In no time, Wally made introductions. She seemed captivated by his crude, socially inept brand of charm and before Tex could snap his fingers, Wally was sweeping the giggly, apple-cheeked woman off to the dance floor.

Tex stared in disbelief. Yep. This was simply too much fun to take in all at once.

He was leaving.

With a dull thud, Charlotte's heart landed in her stomach. While she and Hunt danced, her gaze clung to Tex as he bid first his sisters, and then his aunt and uncle, good-night before heading to the stairs. She stumbled and clutched Hunt's arm for support. She couldn't believe he was leaving so soon. The rat hadn't even asked her to dance.

"Something wrong?"

Charlotte looked guiltily up at Hunt, knowing that the joy had seeped from her expression. "No, I'm just...I don't know. Tired I guess."

"This wouldn't have anything to do with the guy who just left?" Hunt asked, gentle humor lighting his eyes.

"Who?" she asked, feigning ignorance.

Hunt chuckled. "You are going to have to admit it sooner or later."

"Is it that obvious?"

His shoulders bunched. "Well, I didn't want to believe it, for obvious reasons. But you can't fight city hall."

Charlotte heaved a sigh, her smile wan. "You're right. I sure hope I didn't ruin your evening."

"I had a great time. You and the pig are the best dance partners I ever had."

She threw back her head and laughed.

"Want to go home?" Hunt asked.

"Yes, but you don't need to walk with me. There are plenty of security guards everywhere. Not to mention my watch pig." She grinned.

He frowned. "You sure?"

"Yes." Charlotte angled her head toward a group of lovelies in the corner. "Seems to me that one of Tex's sisters has been watching you all evening."

"Me?" He looked genuinely surprised. "No."

"Yes, you."

"Probably just never seen a man square-dance with a pig before."

Again, Charlotte laughed. It was too bad this evening hadn't worked out. Hunt was such a nice man. But he was right. She couldn't get her mind off Tex, and without him, the party had lost its appeal.

As much as Tex didn't want to be around people, he had no desire to go back to the bunkhouse he shared with his cousin Kenny and sit there alone feeling sorry for himself. So, instead, he was raiding Miss Clarise's industrial-sized refrigerator for sandwich makings under the glow of a solitary light bulb and listening to the strains of the rollicking party as they filtered to him through the glass wall. And feeling sorry for himself.

The tempo of the music had changed to a series of slow dance tunes and he hummed along in a forlorn manner as he unloaded the cold-cut drawer.

What a loser. His grim smile was self-deprecating as he threw a Dagwood style sandwich together and slammed the fridge shut with the heel of his boot. Darkness descended once again in the kitchen, matching his mood.

Total loser.

Even Wally had a date for tonight.

Criminy, what a lo-o-oser. Standing here, stuffing his face and wishing that Charlotte would leave the hoedown and search him out.

Fat chance.

As he wrapped his mouth around a giant bite of salami, Swiss, tomato, pickle, lettuce and turkey on sourdough, he could almost swear he glimpsed Charlotte emerging from the barn and heading this way.

Nah.

His eyes were playing tricks on him. It was just wishful thinking. He chewed for a thoughtful moment and then chased the sandwich with ice-cold milk slugged straight from the carton. He stopped. Leaning forward, he squinted out the window again.

Those skirts. Those legs. That cleavage.

That pig.

He watched, mesmerized, as they drew closer. It was

Charlotte all right. And she was coming to the house. To this side of the house. To the door that led to this room. And here he was, a big loser, standing here with mayo all over his face and a milk mustache. Where the hell were the napkins? He wiped his face on his sleeve.

He couldn't let her find him like this, drowning his sorrows in a quart of milk and a homemade sub. Besides, he had absolutely no interest in hearing how much fun she'd had with Hunt. He'd been able to see that with his own eyes.

He glanced about. He had to hide.

Tex grabbed his sandwich and dropped behind the countertop between the refrigerator and the stainless steel island. With a quick glance over his shoulder, he duck-walked toward the door that led to the breakfast room. Knees popping like artillery on the front line, he stilled for a moment, and held his finger to his lips, and then continued. *Pop. Pop. Pop.* For pity's sake, why did his knees have to betray him now? He slowed and before he could make it anywhere near said door, the overhead lights snapped on and the sound of Charlotte's sweet voice filled the room.

"Okay, pig," she murmured.

He froze.

"But just a snack. And then it's off to bed with you. Chocolate you say? Hmm. No. The sugar and caffeine will keep you awake. And, if you're awake, I'm awake."

The tap of Charlotte's heels and clippity-clop of Toto's hooves drew nearer. They were headed to the refrigerator. The refrigerator that Tex was cowering near.

Boy howdy. This evening just kept getting better by the second.

Pop, pop popping, Tex scooted around the corner of the island in the nick of time. He held his breath.

"How about an apple?" Charlotte wondered, as she searched through the fruit drawer. He could hear the sounds of her making a choice and closing the door. "Funny," she muttered. "Some slob didn't clean up after themselves." The silver drawer opened, and she rummaged for a knife.

Toto snuffed and grunted and clippity-clopped around the corner.

Tex closed his eyes.

A cold snout was suddenly pressed to the back of his neck, and Toto squealed with joy.

Tex grabbed the pig's muzzle and fixed him with one of Wally's special gazes. *Shut up,* he telegraphed to the pig. *Don't rat on me, or I'll make sausage out of you.*

Toto seemed impervious to the silent communiqué.

Wally was fired.

Tex held out his sandwich. "Go away," he hissed.

"Toto?" Charlotte called. "Come here, piggy."

Lips smacking, Toto scarfed the sandwich in record time and was now rooting through Tex's clothing, searching for more.

"What are you up to now?" Charlotte sighed. Her skirts rustled as she came looking for Toto.

A bloodcurdling scream rent the air. Clutching her heaving bosom, Charlotte recoiled and, gasping for oxygen, stumbled back toward the refrigerator.

"Auuugghhh! Ohhhh! Aaauuugghhh! Ouchhhh!"

Tex leapt to his feet and caught her just before she fell. "Charlotte, it's me!"

"T-t-tex?"

"Yep," he grunted.

Momentum thus created, together they slammed into the stainless steel refrigerator door and slid to the floor where they landed in a frilly heap.

Chapter Six

"**W**hat in heaven's name are you *doing* here?" Charlotte cried, gasping, flailing, struggling to sort herself from Tex. This was no easy matter, considering the volume of her skirts and the pig that refused to be ignored. "You nearly gave me a heart attack."

Bound together at several key points, she was forced to go with him as he leaned forward to kick the toe of his boot free from the myriad netted layers of petticoat. But it was a mug's game. They were hopelessly entangled.

Tex gave up for a moment to rest. And, seemingly, to enjoy. He batted the ruffles away from his face and blew a wad of lace from between his lips. Lips that were so close she could feel his dimpled, Brubaker grin radiating between their mouths.

"Sorry about that," he murmured. "I didn't mean to scare you."

"It's...I...uh," she tried to lean back, but couldn't.

"Oops. Uh, careful there, my necklace seems to be caught on your button."

"Oh, is *that* the problem? I thought you were thinking I needed mouth-to-mouth or something." The grin broadened.

"Why?" She batted at him and asked saucily, "Are you short of breath?"

"Definitely."

"Probably the fact that I'm practically sitting on your chest, doesn't help matters."

"Pig."

"Well, I beg your pard—"

"No. The *pig*," he grunted, straining to push the reclining Toto off his lap.

"Oh! Toto, come here." Toto obeyed, much to Tex's relief, and came around to sit on Charlotte's lap.

"Uff," they all grunted.

Sitting up the best they could, Tex worked on untangling Charlotte's delicate gold chain from his top button.

"Careful," came her soft advice, "this was my Nanna Dorothy's."

"Then it's very special."

"Mmm-hum."

He glanced up as he worked. "I was the slob who made the sandwich, by the way." His face was a blur.

Her cheeks grew warm. "In the dark?" She leaned back to better see him.

"Careful." Slowly, he disentangled a thread from the knotted links. "Would you believe I was too hungry to take time to turn on the light?"

"No," she guffawed into his face. The nearness of his lips to hers was vastly unsettling. She could feel their breaths mingling, could imagine his lips on hers. "You were sitting on the floor, for pity's sake."

"Would you believe I was too weak from hunger to find a chair?"

"No!" Feeling giddy with proximity, Charlotte's laughter bubbled forth. Still sitting pretty much on top of him, her petticoats crackled and rustled as she turned upon his lap, to give him better access to her throat. Not to be left out, Toto brought his curious snout to their noses, creating a heavily breathing triangle.

"Get the feeling we're not alone?" he joshed.

She giggled and pushed at Toto. "You're stalling. Come on. What's the real reason that you were sitting on the floor in the dark?"

"The truth?"

"Sure, why not?"

His hands stilled for a moment. "Okay. I was hiding from you."

"Hiding from me? Am I that scary?"

"Nope. I was afraid that if we were alone together, I'd be tempted to kiss you again, and since you were on a date with Hunt, I figured I should mind my p's & q's."

"You wanted to kiss me? Even after that lousy first attempt?"

There was a boyish vulnerability in his sigh. "Sorry about that, I guess I'm a little rusty."

"Not *you*, silly. Me! I was the one with the dead lips."

There was a playful mischief in his grin. "They didn't seem so dead to me."

"No?"

"No. But in answer to your question—" he cleared his throat and peered intently at the tangled chain "—yeah. I wanted to kiss you again. But only because I was worried about you."

"Worried?"

"Well, I wanted to make sure that the damage to your

lips wasn't permanent. In case you needed my testimony in a lawsuit or something.'' The tiny links of her necklace were becoming more hopelessly entangled with threads from his top button. She wondered if perhaps he wasn't making it worse on purpose. "Purely scientific," he continued in a most scholarly tone. "Nothing to do with our rather dysfunctional trainer/client relationship, of course."

"Of course." Her neck was beginning to ache, so she leaned her forehead against his. "Anything other than pure, uh—" her words caught in her throat. Oh, his breath tickled her cheeks, and sent waves of goose bumps cascading down her body "—er, science, would be folly, considering we are all wrong for each other."

"Polar opposites. This would be just a kissing cousin thing. An experiment." He glanced up at her with that rakish look that used to make her blood boil. It still did, it seemed, only for different reasons altogether. "One time only."

"Right. Once would most likely do it. That sounds like a…a…very well-thought-out, scientific plan."

"You think so?"

"Sure. After all, you're the researcher."

"That's right. I am. I vote that we do it."

He stopped fumbling with her necklace and slid his fingers to the back of her neck, to create a cradle for her head.

Her heart began to thrum at the pulse points beneath his thumbs. "I was hoping," her sigh was whisper soft, "that you'd give me another chance."

"You were?"

"Mmm. I, um, you know, I, too, simply wanted to make sure everything was back in working order."

"Well, there is only one way to find out."

He released her neck just long enough to push the piles of ruffles—and Toto's quivering snout—from between them and settle her more firmly against his chest. Then, he drew her face near, sought her lips with his and claimed her for his own.

For Charlotte, this kiss was nothing like the kiss they'd shared after the makeup party. This kiss was alive and filled with a passion that she had denied for far too long in her young life. This kiss was more than a simple experiment. It was the portent of things to come for them.

In that regard, Charlotte knew she should probably push Tex away. They'd had their kiss. The experiment was over. Her lips were alive. With the sound of music.

But instead of obeying her head, Charlotte went with the dictates of her heart in this instance. Slowly, like a ballerina executing a graceful dance move, Charlotte lifted her arms and laid them gently over Tex's shoulders and twined her fingers together at his nape.

His hair was oh, so soft, much silkier than it looked, a stark contrast to the rough, five-o'clock shadow that graced his cheeks and chin and abraded her tender cheeks and lips most pleasantly.

Despite the fact that they both knew that they were all wrong for each other, there was nowhere else on this earth that Charlotte would rather be at this moment, than here in Tex's arms. Deep in her throat, she heard herself moan, as he adjusted his position, bringing her body more fully in contact with his. She tugged him closer still and kissed him back with joyful abandon.

"They're working again," she murmured, breaking the kiss long enough to whisper against his lips.

"Hmm?" Again, he closed his mouth over hers, setting her on fire.

"My lips." The words were swallowed by his mouth.

"Mmm." She could tell he agreed.

Charlotte allowed her head to loll back just a bit as he tugged her lower lip into his mouth and nibbled. She giggled and pulled away. "The experiment was—" She was silenced for a moment by another kiss. She finished her sentence on a breathless whoosh "—a success?"

"Mmm. I'd have to agree. But only *you* know if everything is in perfect working order. I'd be willing to stay here with you, and keep working on this—all night, if need be—to make sure that there is absolutely no permanent damage."

The only permanent damage would be to her heart, Charlotte feared, if they kept this up much longer. Already she was in way over her head, emotionally speaking, when it came to Tex Brubaker.

"I think," she sighed, "I'm going to be fine." Very, very fine. Finer than she'd ever been in her life. But, considering how he wanted to keep this on an experimental basis, she felt it would be better not to go into too much detail about the way her toes were curling so tightly she feared she'd never get her shoes off again.

"So." Again, he gently kissed her lips. "You'd give this little test an A?"

"Mmm. Well, yes and no."

"Yes and...*no?*" There was a slight injury in his tone.

"Well, the kiss between us was fine, but I could really live a long time without a potbellied pig snorting in my ear."

Tex glanced at the snuffling Toto and chuckled. "He's just jealous."

"You think?"

"I know." Gently, he traced her lips with the pads of his fingers and then cupped her chin in his hand.

Charlotte had the strangest feeling that there was a

double meaning in those words. And, as much as she reveled in the fact that he might have been a little jealous of Hunt, she knew discussing their feelings in the heat of the moment would not be prudent. Delightful, yes, but dangerous.

Tex was right. They were all wrong for each other. Getting any further involved, other than an experimental kiss, would be foolish. It would be best to nip this budding romance before it got out of hand. She wanted to pursue her freedom. There was plenty of time to fall in love afterward. For far too long, she'd been socially cut off. She wanted to flirt. Do girly things with a passel of girlfriends. Tying herself down to one man at this point in her life would be a big mistake, she told herself, even as she leaned in toward Tex, wishing for another—just one more—mind-blowing kiss.

"So, I suppose Hunt is probably waiting for you. We'd probably better, you know, peel ourselves apart, before he comes gunning for me."

She was surprised at the disappointment she felt at his words.

With ease, Tex stood with Charlotte still in his arms. They stood nose to nose as he tore the top button off his placket and let it dangle from her chain. "A little souvenir from tonight."

"Thanks." Charlotte toyed with the button. "Anyway, you can relax. Hunt and I are not really dating. I simply went with him because he was nice enough to ask."

Ruefully, he glanced down at the hole in his collar placket. "Now you tell me."

She giggled. "Sorry."

"I thought you two were an item."

"Is that why you left without asking me to dance?"

"One of the reasons, yes."

"Oh. Well, I think Hunt might be dancing with one of your sisters, about now."

"In that case, I should probably be the one beating him up."

"That wouldn't be very nice."

"True. Is that why you're back here so early? Because Hunt dumped you for one of my sisters?" Brow arched, grin lopsided, he goaded her.

"He didn't dump me!"

"So you *are* still dating him!"

Charlotte put her hands on his chest and pushed. "You are so weird."

He took her hands and cradled them in his own. "Are you sure your lips are okay? I wouldn't want to take any chances."

"Well, they were tingling a bit, just a little while ago."

"That's a very good sign." He gave her a lazy wink. "How about if we share one slow dance, since I was so inconsiderate and didn't ask at the party. I can hear the music from here."

"Mmm." Charlotte nodded. "Another part of the experiment? Just to make sure that the lipstick didn't affect my ability to dance? Kind of like a complete physical?"

Tex laughed. "Something like that, yeah."

"You should have been a doctor."

"I have been known to play a doctor."

"On TV?"

"No. Back when I was five. With the neighbor girl."

"Naughty, naughty," Charlotte giggled as they took a turn around the linoleum.

"That's what she said."

Charlotte could not sleep. Whether from the racket of the party, or from the aftereffects of Tex's good-night kisses, she couldn't be sure. Although, if she had to guess, it was Tex's kisses.

"Ohhh," she moaned and shoved her pillow off the bed. This was getting her nowhere. *Sleep,* she commanded herself, and tried to count sheep, but instead found herself counting the number of kisses she'd shared with Tex in front of her door before he'd finally headed for home. It had been a goodly amount, that was for sure. Hot, exciting kisses that turned her insides to overcooked linguini. Never had she been kissed like that before.

And, she doubted she ever would be again.

After all, it had been nothing but a scientific experiment, carried a bit too far.

Once again, Charlotte forced herself to remember that she was enjoying her freedom. She didn't need another person in her life, telling her what to do. To feel. To think.

Nanna Dorothy had spent ten years trying to control her and that was enough. Charlotte needed time to simply be on her own. At nobody's constant beck and call. Although, she mused, being at Tex's beck and call would certainly be different than Nanna's. No! She couldn't allow her thoughts to go in that direction. She was free. She wanted to stay that way. Didn't she? Besides, she and Tex had absolutely nothing in common. He'd said so himself. Except for maybe the nuclear fission that seemed to happen every time their lips made contact.

Charlotte kicked her legs and flung off her covers. One thing was certain. Lying here in the darkness, listening to Toto snore and indulging in useless fantasy was pure torture. Swinging her legs over the mattress's edge, she sat up and flipped on her nightstand light. No way could she sleep.

There was a mountain of paperwork she could be sorting through at Nanna Dorothy's. The night was still relatively young. Nanna Dorothy's was only ten minutes away by car. She could run over there, forget Tex, make a routine security check of the doors and windows, not think about Tex, sort through the mail, collect whatever bills needed paying, ignore these incessant thoughts of Tex, listen to the answering machine and see how many Realtors had left cards on the counter after showing the house.

And, she could still probably be back here by midnight—or shortly thereafter—having completely purged Tex from her thoughts.

Perfect.

She pulled on some jeans, a pair of tennis shoes, and a T-shirt. Then, she twisted her hair up into a ponytail, powdered her nose, dabbed on a bit of makeup, brushed her teeth and called to her pig.

Charlotte loved Nanna Dorothy's old Georgian-style mansion. At one time, it had been the main house on a sprawling plantation. But now, the cul-de-sacs and tract divisions had crowded in on the old girl, making her look rather out of place. The newer houses were all very nice, but still, the mansion stuck out like a cocktail dress at a church social. And now, she looked especially forlorn with the single light burning on the front porch and the For Sale sign listing slightly to the left in the front lawn.

As Charlotte parked and assisted Toto out of her car, she could hear the familiar night sounds she used to enjoy when she lived here with Nanna Dorothy. The crickets song, the rustle of leaves as the light summer breezes whispered by, the far-off sounds of the city—

"Maaaa! Maaaa!"

And the bleat of the Martkowskis' goat?

Charlotte frowned. Daisy Mae was a little more exuberant than usual, especially for this time of night.

"Daisy Mae, hush up," she hissed and headed to the front porch.

Daisy Mae seemed to have no intention of hushing and only redoubled her attention-getting efforts.

"Maaaa! Maaaa! Maaaa!"

Blasted goat. "Toto, get back over here. She just wants attention." Attention that the people who owned her should be giving her. With a disgusted shake of her head, she jammed her key into the lock and pushed open Nanna Dorothy's front door.

"Maaa! Maaa!"

Were these people deaf? That constant bleating was going to drive her nuts. They must have forgotten to feed the silly thing. Well, hopefully they'd wake up and feed her, because over here, the cupboards were bare of goat fare, and she was fresh out of tin cans and license plates.

"Maaaaaaaaaaaaaaa!"

After a long, soulful glance at the fence that separated the two yards, Toto slipped inside after Charlotte. "Daisy Mae! Shut up!" she shouted, and closed the door behind her with a resounding slam.

The familiar scents of lilacs and lemon furniture polish brought back an instant flood of memories, and Charlotte felt the tears spring unbidden into her eyes. She missed Nanna Dorothy. For as crotchety and ill-tempered as she could be at times, Charlotte knew that the ancient lady had loved her without reserve.

She laid her purse and keys on the small table in the foyer and gathered up a pile of mail that lay under the slot in the front door. After tucking the bundle next to her purse, she stepped from room to room flipping on lights. From beyond the windows, Daisy Mae could be heard whipping herself into a frenzy.

What kind of idiot would choose a goat for a pet in the suburbs? Yes, the Martkowskis had a big lawn, but was it really worth the trouble to keep a goat, when a lawn mower was much less labor intensive? Not to mention easier on the eardrums at this time of night.

From the kitchen, Charlotte collected several paper grocery bags and headed to the den to begin loading them with files and paperwork that she could sort in her room at Miss Clarise's place. It was much less lonely and the memories were not there to overwhelm her.

"Maaaaa! Maaaaa!"

Daisy Mae's racket made it difficult to open the safe. She had to try the combination three times, before the heavy door swung open. Inside the safe, Charlotte found the typical documents, Nanna Dorothy's birth certificate, passport, the deed to the house, the cars, the boat, the summer place, some newspaper articles from way back, keys to heaven only knew what, some photo negatives, a stack of cash, and an envelope that indicated the contents should be read upon Nanna Dorothy's death.

Odd.

"Maaaaa! Maaaaaaaaaaaaa!"

What was this? Charlotte pried open the metal wings that held the flap in place and dumped the contents on Nanna Dorothy's old marble and cherry desk.

"Mmmmmmmmmaaaaaaaaaaaaaaaaaa!"

A videotape? What on earth? Charlotte held up the papers and began to read.

"Mmmmmmaaaaaaaaaaaaaaaaaaaaaaaaaaaaaaaaaaa!"

Exasperated beyond measure, Charlotte tossed the papers back into the envelope after the video, threw the whole thing into the safe and slammed the door. That did it. She was going to go out there and give those brain-dead neighbors a piece of her mind.

"Come on, pig," she gritted out, and marched back through the front foyer, down the porch steps across the driveway, up the neighbors' walk, to their door where she leaned on the doorbell. Repeatedly.

No answer.

She pounded. She shouted. She pounded some more. Still no answer.

The lights across the street, however, came on. Mrs. Donnely poked her curlered head out the door.

"Hi, Mrs. Donnely, it's me, Charlotte."

"Hello, dear. I thought maybe the Martkowskis were being robbed."

And the robber was knocking? Charlotte smiled at the ditzy Mrs. Donnely. "No, ma'am. I was just trying to let them know that their goat is needing some attention."

"Oh? I wish they'd get rid of that horrible thing. Anyway, you won't find them home for a week or so, dear. Maybe longer. They left for vacation day before yesterday."

"Vacation? Okay. Thanks."

Mrs. Donnely slipped back inside, clearly not interested in helping to rescue Daisy Mae.

Vacation? Charlotte rolled her eyes. She guessed it was up to her to help the dumb thing. Hanging around Tex had made her heart go flabby, when it came to animals. Before meeting him, she may have been tempted to ignore Daisy Mae's pleas for help.

Then again, perhaps not.

"Maaaaaaaaaaaa!" Daisy Mae sounded truly distressed.

Tex had finally drifted off to sleep, when the jangle of his nightstand phone jolted him to consciousness.

"Tex?"

"Hmm?" *Charlotte?* He fumbled for the clock. After midnight.

"It's me, Charlotte."

"Mmm." He smiled. A little pillow talk was always welcome.

"Tex," her voice was breathless, "I need you! You have to come here, right away."

He sat up and raised a brow. This was getting interesting. It was a bit more aggressive than he'd have expected from Charlotte, but he wasn't going to quibble. Especially considering the dream he'd just been having. "Uh, okay. Just give me a second to wake up here."

"Tex, have you got a pencil?"

This question was from out in left field. A pencil. He blinked. What was a pencil again? Oh, yeah. "Uh, sure. Just a sec." He rummaged in his nightstand drawer. "Got a pencil."

"Good. Write down these directions."

Tex had to scribble on an old envelope for all he was worth to keep up with her, but when she was finished, he had the vague notion that this was not a romantic rendezvous. The list she'd dictated was his first clue.

A bunch of old newspapers.

A galvanized tub.

Several blankets.

A first-aid kit and...

Goat food?

Tex screeched to a stop in front of the address that Charlotte had given him and grabbing as many supplies as he could hold, rushed to the backyard. "What happened?" he called, spotting Charlotte kneeling near what looked to be a doghouse. He dropped down next to her and spotted a mother goat lying on the ground, and two babies, looking rather listless, lying nearby.

Cheeks streaked with tears, her words tumbled out in a jumbled rush. "This is Daisy Mae. Her owners are on vacation, and I found her nearly hanging by her tether. It got tangled around her house and wound around that pole over there and it took me until just now to get her loose.

"I'm guessing her babies are newborn, but I'm no expert. I couldn't find any water, and her food was gone, and oh, Tex, she just looked so miserable. How could someone leave their pregnant goat tied up this way, with no food, or no water and in this heat. The babies are so little—" her voice failed her.

Tex shook his head. "It happens all the time."

There was a quiver in her voice. "Really?"

"Mmm-humm. Unfortunately, they don't all have a caring neighbor like you to save the day."

"Will she be all right?"

"I think she's gonna be fine. We can sit here with her for a while, and get her all fixed up, and then we can come back in the morning to check on her."

"I'm thinking of just spending the night here."

Tex bowed his head to hide his blooming grin. The Charlotte he'd met so many weeks ago would never have considered spending the night somewhere in order to keep an eye on an ailing goat. Perhaps there was hope for them after all.

"I could stay with you, if you like?"

"Would you do that?"

"Sure. If you make some coffee."

"Nanna Dorothy has some instant."

"Fine."

Charlotte pushed herself to a standing position, then

bent to run a hand over his hair. "Thank you," she whispered.

Their gazes caught and held, sparking in the shadows. Both were remembering the kisses they'd shared earlier.

"Anytime," he assured her.

"I'll…uh, I'll just go get that coffee."

It was going to be a long night.

Daisy Mae and her babies were resting comfortably now in a soft nest of crumpled newspaper, old pillows and some beach blankets found in Nanna's garage. Daisy Mae hadn't had much of an appetite, but she'd drunk like a sailor on shore leave from the bowl of water they'd provided, then plopped down next to her two babies and—after checking them over and finding them satisfactory—fell sound asleep.

Two Adirondack chairs from the Martkowskis' deck, some hand-crocheted afghans from Nanna Dorothy's place and a TV tray holding a thermos of coffee and a tin of cookies had transformed the Martkowskis' backyard into a cozy piece of heaven, as far as Charlotte was concerned.

It wasn't exactly cold outside, but the breeze had a bit of a kick to it, and Charlotte was glad for the afghans. And for Tex's warm fingers twined with her own. The full moon had risen high in the sky and that—along with a single flaming tiki torch—nicely illuminated the area with a soft romance. Midnight shadows flickered as they sat near the little goat's house, talking in soothing whispers.

"So you were an only child?" His chin cupped in his free palm, Tex regarded Charlotte with that lazy, sexy look that had her stomach knotting with excitement.

"Umm-hm. But I didn't really know any better. My

parents were very busy people. They both taught school overseas. My mother was a teacher and my father was a principal. I went to boarding high school, so I always felt like I had a boatload of siblings. I just never really felt like I had any parents.'' Her sigh was somewhat rueful.

"Were you lonely?"

"Mmm, yes and no. My parents taught on a base in another city, so I got to see them some weekends and on holidays. But, luckily for me, Nanna Dorothy visited often. When she was younger, back in her late seventies and early eighties—'' Charlotte grinned at Tex's chuckle "—she was really spry. You'd have loved her. Anyway, she really took me under her wing. I think she sensed that I was lonely and awkward and yearning for attention. She would call me all the time and write the most wonderful letters, and was always there for me at Christmas and my birthday. She was a surrogate mother.''

"You were lucky to have her.''

"Oh, yes. That's why, when her health began to fail, as she reached ninety and just as I was graduating from high school, there was no question in my mind that I would be there for her. Especially since my parents had passed on while I was still in high school, my mother from pneumonia and my father from cancer just months afterward.''

"You had a tough childhood.''

"Well, I had to grow up fast, in any event, yes.''

"If you and Nanna Dorothy were so close, don't you ever wonder why she handled her last will and testament the way she did?''

Charlotte shrugged the afghan up over her shoulder and lolled her head to better cast her sleepy gaze on Tex. "Oh, I don't know. Nanna Dorothy was always full of surprises. Even at a hundred years old, she was a real corker. Sometimes so cranky you'd like to scream, but for the most part, she was a hoot. Loved a practical joke. I'm sure that's why I got the pig. I'm not sure what the entire reason is, yet, but so far, owning Toto has proved to be much more interesting than I'd originally have thought it would be.''

Tucking his chin to his shoulder, Tex allowed his gaze to rove her face, a curious combination of lazy interest in his eyes.

"We'd never have met, if it hadn't been for that pig."

"True."

"That would have been a crying shame."

He brought her fingers to his mouth and pressed them to his lips. Such soft, warm lips. Lips that she longed to press to her own. But she couldn't do that. The experiment was over. He'd think she'd used the goats as a ruse, to drag him out here in the middle of the night to take up where they'd left off.

Not that that wasn't a wonderful idea. But still, her freedom was at stake here. She allowed her eyes to slide shut and simply enjoyed the feeling of her fingers on his lips. Inside his lips. Mmmm. She could certainly get used to this.

"So," she murmured, hoping to settle her raging pulse. If she engaged him in conversation, he couldn't suck on her fingers in that thoroughly distracting way. That way that turned her insides to liquid passion. "So…" she cleared her throat, "uh, you have a lot of brothers and sisters."

"Yep."

He held her fingertips against his mouth as he spoke and there was something so sensual about the simple gesture. Eyes closed, she concentrated on the hedonistic delights.

Charlotte laughed. "I still can't get over the fact that you're all named after states. What a funny way to name your kids."

He pulled her hand to his heart and covered it with his own. "If you think that's funny, my dad's and Uncle Big Daddy's other two brothers named their kids after cars and calendar months."

"Good grief! How many of you Brubakers are there, altogether, anyway?"

"Well, it's not too hard keeping 'em all straight, if you just remember that Big Daddy, who's my father's older brother, is a huge fan of country music. Big Daddy has nine kids, all named after country western singers."

"Right. I knew about...let's see," she held up her fingers and began to tick off names, "there's Conway, Merle, Buck, and Patsy, and uh, Johnny, Kenny, the twins, Waylon and Willie and little Hank! Although, I guess he's not so little anymore."

"He's out of high school now."

"Right. Nanna Dorothy used to talk about them so much I felt as if I were growing up with them. I used to pretend I was their long-lost other sister, Dotty."

"You'd have fit right in, with that name." He dimpled.

"Tell me about your other cousins."

"Well, Big Daddy and my dad have two younger brothers, Buford who named his kids after cars, Ford, Chevy, Dodge, Porsche and Mercedes, and then there was their youngest brother Harlan, who named his kids after months; April, May, June, July, Augustus and Jason."

"Jason?"

"Stands for July, August, September, October and November. His mother drew the line when Uncle Harlan wanted to name him September. There are other branches of the Brubaker family tree, in other states, with other crazy names, but I can never seem to keep 'em all straight.''

Charlotte giggled. ''I suppose you're going to name your kids after famous animals or something goofy like that.''

''You mean like Flipper and Silver and the twins, Lassie and Rin Tin-Tin?''

''I suppose Flipper is a gymnast?''

''Of course.''

They laughed.

The evening waxed and waned with lazy conversation and all too soon, the first rays of dawn were filtering over the eastern fence. For many wonderful hours, Charlotte had lain slumped against the arm of the Adirondack chair, helpless with laughter, as Tex regaled her with wild tales of a youth spent with eight precocious siblings.

''I'm jealous,'' she finally said, pushing herself upright and swiping at the tears of hilarity in her eyes. ''As an only child, I always wanted a little brother or sister.''

''Yeah? Well, there were days I wanted to be an only child. Grass is always greener, I expect.''

Charlotte stared into his eyes, wondering if her commitment to freedom was really greener than a commitment to a living, breathing, man.

Again, she questioned the wisdom of trying to keep Tex at arms' length. The idea of life without him seemed less appealing all the time.

Chapter Seven

For the next week, Charlotte threw herself into researching the Action-Adventure Clothier Company, ordering her starter kit, and organizing another party for that Friday night. Twice a day, she drove out to the Martkowskis' to take care of Daisy Mae and the kids, who were recovering nicely and frolicking about the Martkowskis' fenced-in back lawn with carefree abandon. Daisy Mae had pretty much decimated their garden, but Charlotte felt it served them right. There was no way she was going to tie that goat up again, and chance her hanging herself while the owners were away.

When she wasn't working on her clothing business, or taking care of Daisy Mae, she worked with Toto, fine-tuning his training and scouring the Internet for the current 411 on potbellied pigs and seeing-eye guide dogs. Something about that whole thing interested her, for some reason.

Then, there were her ten o'clock classes with Tex and Toto. Those were fraught with an undercurrent of sexual tension that turned such mundane topics as a goat's diet into electrifying conversation. Even so, she did her best to keep her distance from the captivating Tex. They hadn't shared another kiss since the night of the hoedown. And, though the cravings for his touch were pretty much a constant, dull ache, she was relieved to a degree.

She needed time to think about what was happening between them. For so long they'd been like gunpowder and fire, their explosive relationship fraught with unrest.

And now? They were like gunpowder and fire.

Still.

"Kitty, sit." Kitty wobbled across the training area and slumped across Charlotte's feet. "No, you gooneybird." She arranged the floppy animal into a sitting position. "Wike dat, silly willy." Prattling away in baby-speak, she didn't notice Tex come up behind her.

"What book you learn dat from, wittle girl?"

"Oh, hi!" Flush-faced, Charlotte straightened and patted at the strands of hair that had escaped her bun. "Actually, you'd be proud of me."

"You've decided to adopt a wife for Toto and go into the pig training business?"

"Hardly. No, I've been reading one of the periodicals on your desk on how to train seeing-eye dogs."

"Why?"

"Just killing time until you got here, I guess. Nanna Dorothy was nearly blind, so it—" she shrugged "—you know, interests me."

"You're early today," he said, getting down to business.

"Yeah, I have to leave early. I'm hosting my first Action-Adventure Clothier party tonight."

"Back in the saddle, huh?"

"So to speak. I'm a little nervous, after last week's fiasco."

"You'll do fine."

"You think?"

"Yeah. I think you do fine at whatever you set your mind to."

"Except makeup sales."

"Wasn't your fault."

She glanced up at him. "You're sweet."

"Just telling the truth."

They stood for the longest moment, recalling that evening. That kiss. The kisses that followed. The kisses they were yearning for now, but in which they could not allow themselves to indulge. It was with an ever-gnawing sense of frustration that Tex called to the pig, and began putting him through his paces.

That evening Tex came into his office, took one look around, strode to the wall calendar and began counting the days until the end of Wally's term. Thirteen days—his gaze shifted to the clock—six hours, twenty-four minutes and thirty...twenty-nine...twenty-eight...seconds.

And not a second too soon. Slowly, he turned and sagged against the wall. With his forefinger and thumb, he pinched the bridge of his nose and then squinted once again at the bomb shelter that had once been his office.

"Wally?"

"Yeah, boss," came the distracted reply.

"What the hell is all this stuff?" he demanded, sweeping his arm around the room and indicating the beakers and burners and books that completely obliterated the Formica of his countertops. "It stinks."

Wally glanced up then buried his nose back in the

book he'd been rapidly highlighting. "Part of my chemistry final."

"Why can't you do this stuff at your place?"

"My roommate can't take the smell."

"I can see why! Listen, if you are going to use my office as a chemistry lab, at least do the stinky stuff in the back storeroom, okay?"

"Okay," Wally murmured.

"How are you coming with that paper?"

Eyes blank, Wally stared at him.

Tex huffed in noisy disgust. "The article we agreed you'd write? Back at the beginning of the term? The one I need for the conference in Houston?"

"Oh, right. It's coming, boss. I'll be starting it soon."

"You haven't *started* it?" Tex gestured to an overflowing pile of papers and textbooks. "You mean this is not your paper? What is it?"

"More homework." Wally slammed his book shut, capped his yellow marker and jumped off his stool. With a quick adjustment of his pants, he shuffled to the door.

"Where are you going?"

"I have a date." Wally grinned. "Mona. That chick I met at the hoedown."

Chick? Wally referred to this woman as a chick, and yet she wanted to go out with him? Now Tex was really depressed. Even the scatterbrained, socially inept doofus Wally had a love life.

That did it.

It was Friday night, and he would not spend another lonely evening in the company of a bunch of dogs and horses and pigs. He was going to Charlotte's Action-Adventure Clothier party. To do a little shopping.

But not necessarily for clothes.

* * *

Charlotte was wheeling a cart full of the last of her Action-Adventure Clothier supplies to the parlor, when she ran into Tex in the hallway that evening.

"What are you doing here, Tex?" she hissed, casting a nervous glance into the filled-to-bursting parlor. It seemed that word had spread about her last party, and the curious had multiplied. There had to be nearly a hundred people milling about and finding seats. Folding chairs were spilling out the archways and into the dining room and foyer.

Good for business. Bad for Charlotte's nerves.

"I was bored, and so I thought I'd come watch your show."

She stared at him. *He* was going to be watching her, too? She was going to be sick.

He must have been able to see the panic in her eyes, because he put a soothing arm around her shoulders, and rubbed her upper arm. "You have nothing to worry about this time. You've had plenty of time to rehearse—"

"But what if I'm not polished enough? Already, I can't seem to remember my lines," she wailed, pressing her face into his shoulder. "I don't think I'm cut out for sales."

"Honey, you can't let one little disaster hold you back. You are a fighter, Charlotte Beauchamp. That's one of the things I love about you."

She pulled her face off his shirt and stared up at him. "It is?" she asked dazedly.

"Yep. One of the many things."

Love?

Did he say love? Did he say he loved *many* things about her? And, had he just called her honey?

Head swimming, she gazed up at him, her eyes glazed over, her mouth gaping. For pity's sake, why did he have to choose this moment to mess with her mind? Heaven only knew what he meant by this offhand comment. Most likely, it was simply a friendly reassurance. Then again…

Realizing a tad too late that she must have looked absolutely addlebrained, she forced a smile.

"So, you're going to stay?" she chirped.

"Yep. Thought I'd do some shopping."

One of Tex's sisters was sitting within earshot and hooted. "Hear that, girls?" she asked the other three. "Brother Tex is going to do some clothes shopping."

Tex's sisters all burst out laughing.

"Keep it up and I'll cross you four off my list," he threatened with a grin. Brandishing a playful fist, he moved to squeeze in the middle of their sofa, a lanky tumbleweed in the middle of the flower patch. They all whispered and teased, the way siblings did, in that secret language that Charlotte had never quite understood.

Gripping her cart, Charlotte—her plastic smile still in place—moved through the crowd, dazedly rolling over the toes of expensive shoes and thwacking the stocking-clad knees and shins of her potential customers.

There were things about her that Tex loved?

What things?

Thunderstruck, she bumbled her way through the throng, and then as if floating along in slow motion, set up her displays, charts, samples and brochures. She passed out the ordering blanks and size and color literature, and noted, with a furtive peek, that Tex studied this information with interest. What was with this guy? She did not know any man who would take the time to give this stuff a second glance. Unless—Charlotte took a deep, steadying breath—unless he really was beginning to fall for her?

She glanced up and suddenly found herself caught in

the swirling vortex of his gaze. A slow smile tugged at his lips and he gave her the laziest of winks. Heart throbbing, stomach roiling, she backed into the display table and ricocheted from there to the podium Miss Clarise had set up for her convenience. The speakers shrieked as she drew too close to the microphone. The room became tomblike in its silence.

Show time.

Later, when she had time, she would analyze the meaning of the word *love,* within the context that Tex had used. Gracious. He couldn't be falling for her. They were all wrong for each other. Oh well. She'd figure it out some other time. Right now, she would simply concentrate on not fainting.

"The wonder of Action-Adventure Clothing is that it is multifunctional."

Thumbs up, Tex nodded and smiled broadly, hoping to encourage Charlotte as she once again, struggled awkwardly through another company introduction and product spiel.

"We at...er, uh, um, Action-Adventure Clothiers believe it is important to be prepared for any eventuality. With Action-Adventure Clothing, you can be ready for any occasion at a moment's notice. With the clothing in this one tiny carryall—" she held up the sample bag "—I'll show you how you can go from a hike in the woods to the office to the dance floor, by simply rotating your...uh...pieces, and of course, accessorizing! The beauty of Action-Adventure is that one size fits all."

There was a murmur among the audience. Brows were furrowed, arched, knitted with puzzlement. *All?* they seemed to wonder.

"Yes, one size fits all! Isn't that marvelous?" Charlotte muttered as she sorted through her clothing kit for the starter pieces. "If EttaMae Hanson, our plus-sized model, will please step forward, we can begin."

"I'm not gonna undress in front of him," EttaMae grumped, pointing at Tex.

The women all tittered.

Tex grinned. "Take it off, EttaMae!" he shouted good-naturedly, attempting to loosen things up. Charlotte looked about as skittish as an unbroken colt.

A wave of laughter rippled throughout the room.

EttaMae colored girlishly and batted the air in his direction. "In your dreams, sonny boy."

"No need to worry, everyone, EttaMae will be able to do all of her changing right here, and still remain modest," Charlotte called over the gaiety.

Tex could see that her hands were trembling as she fumbled with her start-up kit.

"This fabulous carryall, when fully unzipped, unbuttoned and unVelcroed, also serves as a strapless sundress, or a full-length skirt, or a bathing suit cover-up. In a matter of moments, you can be ready for anything. It's easy as one..." She fumbled with the snaps and zippers for a moment. "Two..." She consulted the directions and tried again. "Three. Hmm. EttaMae, could you hold this end?" she asked, shoving half of the bag into her model's hands. Charlotte tugged and pried and wrestled with the various fasteners, to no avail. "I don't understand," she murmured, her face flushing a deep crimson, "It worked beautifully this afternoon up in my room."

Tex held up his hand. "Toss it over here, babe. I'm good at unzipping women's clothes."

"Ooooooo!" Throughout the room, women giggled and teased and heckled the only man present.

Tex gave his head a rakish waggle and waved at the smiling crowd.

With a shrug, Charlotte tossed him the bag and reaching up, he effortlessly fielded it. His sisters leaned across him on the couch, crowding around to assist.

"While we wait for Tex, we can move on to the Action-Adventure bra."

"I ain't tryin' no bra on in front of him!" EttaMae roared.

Charlotte pulled a tissue from her pocket and dabbed at her brow. "Good enough. We'll move on to the hiking/ evening gear. EttaMae—" Charlotte picked up her scripted notes and began to read "—I'll bet one of your favorite leisure activities is hiking."

"No. Hate it."

"Oh? Okay. Uh, er…well. Umm…" Charlotte frantically read ahead. "And when you're not hiking, you enjoy the occasional cocktail party—"

"Never. Fuzzy and me watch TV. He operates the remote, I knit."

The alarming sounds of fabric ripping came from the vicinity of Tex's couch. He and his sisters all looked up, guilty expressions on their faces.

"Oops," he muttered.

All heads swiveled to Charlotte.

"Never mind," she chirped, flipping through her cue cards for phase two of the show. "We have another dress that can go from day to evening with the addition of our elastic belt collection."

Charlotte unfurled what looked to Tex like an oversized tablecloth, gathered with elastic at the top.

"This is our Action-Adventure shift/skirt/cocktail dress that we call the 'Everything dress.' It's flame retardant, waterproof, airtight and can work in an emergency situation as a tent or parachute.'' Charlotte did a double take at her notes. ''Yes, that's what it says. However—'' she cast a nervous smile at the curmudgeonly EttaMae ''—considering that you enjoy indoor activities, this is probably not a selling point.''

''Yeah, I'd leave the word 'tent' out of your little spiel in the future,'' EttaMae agreed.

''Good idea. Forget I said that,'' Charlotte advised the audience. To EttaMae she asked, ''Ready?''

''As I'll ever be.'' EttaMae sounded about as excited as Eeyore.

Charlotte draped the yards of fabric over EttaMae's frizzy head and instructed, ''EttaMae, you can take your clothes off now.''

''I ain't takin' my clothes off in front of him,'' came the muffled reply. From under the voluminous folds, EttaMae's finger poked in Tex's direction.

''Take it off, EttaMae,'' Tex shouted.

More laughter.

''It's okay, EttaMae, we can't see a thing.''

Grudgingly, EttaMae complied and her blouse finally appeared from the top of the skirt. Her skirt followed and Tex whistled. EttaMae's head poked through the neck hole and she scowled at Tex, but it was obvious she enjoyed the attention.

''All right now.'' Charlotte pulled EttaMae's bare arms out and settled the top of the baggy dress under her armpits. Charlotte could see how the Everything dress could indeed work as a tent.

A sweat broke out on her brow. This was going to be just a trifle more difficult than she'd envisioned. EttaMae looked like a bag of oatmeal.

Belts! That's what this ensemble needed. Belts and matching shoes.

Charlotte glanced up at Tex. He was smiling. All of a sudden she was grateful for his steadying presence. She could do this. Tex thought she could. He'd said she was capable of accomplishing anything she set her mind to, and that was true, although, untangling the belts was something she should have thought of beforehand. After a tense moment, she finally had them sorted and began to apply them to EttaMae.

Caesar. Now EttaMae looked like Caesar. All she needed was a laurel wreath on her head, and she'd be the spitting image. All at once, Rome began to burn in her mind's eye. The room had gone quiet. Women changed the angle of their heads, as if trying to find the redeeming qualities in this new look. Some folks whispered. Some giggled. EttaMae looked distinctly unhappy. The bare-armed toga look was not for her, that was obvious to everyone. The question that remained?

Who was the toga look for?

Sensing Charlotte's distress, Miss Clarise once again saved the day by announcing intermission and herding her guests to the dining room for a sumptuous dessert repast, complete with a champagne fountain.

"You didn't have to follow me out here to Nanna Dorothy's. I'm perfectly safe."

"I know. I just wanted to check up on the goat."

"Oh, sure," she sniffed, clearly not believing him.

Tex dropped into the Adirondack chair next to the one where Charlotte was slumped and reached for her hand. It was obvious that she'd been crying as she sat here all alone—with the exception of the drowsy barnyard life—in the Martkowskis' backyard. The sun had set hours ago, and a cloud cover obliterated most of the moon's glow. The flickering light of the tiki torch was the only illumination, but it was enough for Tex to see the tear stains on her cheeks.

"So, how's she doing?" He inclined his head in Daisy Mae's direction.

"Fine. I think she's a good listener."

Tex nodded. "I find most animals to be."

"I never knew that."

"Yeah. They don't interrupt. They don't give advice. They don't judge. They just listen."

"Kind of like you."

"You callin' me an animal?"

Her smile was watery and she hiccuped. "It's a compliment."

"Charlotte Beauchamp, I do believe you are getting to be an old softy, when it comes to our furry friends."

"And our not-so-furry ones."

She was scratching Toto's head when she spoke, but he couldn't be sure that she wasn't talking about him. In any event, he decided to change the subject to keep from standing and pulling her into his arms. Charlotte needed a friend. Not someone to take advantage of her when her defenses were down.

"You made some sales tonight, after you left."

"You mean after I ran away."

"You didn't run away. Everyone understood about your splitting headache."

Skeptical, Charlotte lifted her brow. "Who would be stupid enough to buy clothes from me after that inept demonstration?"

"Well, I for one, did some Christmas shopping."

"For who? Some of your cattle? Those clothes weren't meant for the human body."

The comical expression on her face had him welling with laughter. "That's not true. I think part of your problem was your choice of model. EttaMae's mean lookin' face was enough to stall even the most impulsive of the impulse buyers. Why did you choose her, anyway?''

Charlotte lifted a shoulder. ''I don't know. She just seems like the average woman.''

''Honey, EttaMae isn't even the average bear.'' Tex was glad to see the shadow of a smile grace her lips. ''Anyway, after you left, several of the ladies began to try on your samples and they were great. Miss Clarise kept the records, but I think you had a pretty good night.''

''Really?'' She lifted a listless hand and her smile was wan. ''Miss Clarise is such a doll. Even so, I think I'm going to throw in the towel on clothing sales. I don't think the fashion world is ready for me.''

''Why not?''

''It's just a vague, uneasy feeling.'' She squirmed in her chair to better face him and looked up at him with a quiet intensity that pulled his gaze deep into her own. Her words were filled with passion. ''Tex, I know that there is something out there for me. Something fulfilling. Something exciting. Something that I'm really good at and that I'll love. It's simply a matter of finding out what it is, and then going for it.''

Off in the distance, the steady drone of crickets' song serenaded them. Several doors down, a dog barked. The sleepy sounds of suburbia winding down for the night filtered to them, but Tex didn't notice, so focused was he on the sweet tones of Charlotte's voice.

''Yeah,'' he finally sighed. ''Finding work you love is very important.''

Nearly as important as finding a person to love. His gaze dropped to her hands as she absently scratched the little pig who sat at her feet. Could Charlotte be the one for him? More and more, he was beginning to wonder. Tex stretched out and crossed his legs at the ankles. Propping his chin in his hands, he peered through the shifting shadows at the woman curled at his side.

She had no idea that within a few short months, she'd turned his entire world on its ear. And it worried him. For as much as he was committed to his work, he wondered if he wouldn't give it all up for Charlotte Beauchamp.

"You've had kind of a rough time of it lately, and I was thinking, since it's Saturday, maybe we could take the day off. I know you want to get Toto trained as quickly as possible, but trust me, a day off will do us all a world of good."

It was the morning after her Action-Adventure Clothier fiasco and Charlotte was feeling lower than a worm in a ditch. She glanced blearily over the edge of her coffee mug to catch the hopeful look in Tex's eyes. A tiny smile began to steal across her lips, nudging the melancholy away.

He had to be a mind reader. Putting Toto through his paces that morning was the last thing she felt like doing. After the previous night's fashion debacle, she wanted nothing more than to dig a hole out in the pasture and bury her head. But a day off with Tex would be eminently more satisfying and far less messy. Leaning back in her club chair, she regarded him as he sat sprawled behind his desk, feet crossed comfortably atop his ink blotter.

"What did you have in mind?"

He bunched his shoulders and tipped his head. "I was thinking we could take the pig and the puppy on a little trip. Head down to the pond in front of the bunkhouses. Go for a swim. Have a picnic. Relax.''

Swimming in the pond with Tex instead of training her pig? Sounded heavenly. Though she knew she should decline the invitation in the interest of preserving what was left of her sanity, she ignored the warning voice in the back of her mind. The rational voice that fairly shouted, *"This man is not for you. Run. Head for the hills. Freedom awaits."*

"I love it. When do we leave?"

His eyes widened with surprised pleasure. "Uh, well, I guess as soon as you go get your swimsuit."

"I'm wearing it." She'd planned to go for a swim in Miss Clarise's pool right after today's lesson, so she'd worn her suit under her shorts.

"In that case—" he stood, eager to be on his way "—after you."

The midmorning sun was already driving up the mercury as Tex—carrying the puppy—led her and Toto down toward the stables. Charlotte figured that's where he'd parked his big, comfortable Jeep with the leather seats and the expensive sound system.

When Tex had suggested that they ride out the mile or so to his place on horseback instead, she'd been too stunned to argue. Fighting the anxiety she felt about her first horse ride, she followed him to the paddock in silence.

The horses that milled within were huge.

Her fears grew in direct proportion to the animal's size.

How he found joy in working with such intimidating beasts continued to mystify her. She took the puppy from him, then trailed him with her gaze as he climbed through the split rails. For an instant, he disappeared inside the stable to select some gear from the tack room. Upon returning, he gave a low whistle, sectioned out a horse from the group and bridled it with swift efficiency. Struck by the power and confidence he exuded, Charlotte watched as his muscles rippled beneath the faded fabric of a snug navy T-shirt. The horse sensed his authority. Patiently, the large animal stood as Tex lifted the saddle off the fence rail with an ease born of years of practice. The economy of movement was truly poetry in motion. She could stand here and watch him work this way all day.

Charlotte inhaled deeply.

Tex was a man's man. Tough. Hard. Strong.

Even so, she couldn't help but notice that he was not the same man who'd barreled in on her visit with Miss Clarise earlier that summer. Slowly, their relationship had mellowed. Matured. The Tex she now knew was strong, yes, but also funny and kind, sensitive and understanding.

And, when he held her and kissed her, all rational thought left her head.

A woman would be incredibly lucky to call him her own.

The realization that she was staring at him all moony-eyed jolted Charlotte back to the present and she commanded herself to stop allowing her thoughts to stray to Tex this way. Deliberately, she forced her gaze away from him and focused on the pig that lay upon his boots as he tightened cinch straps and checked the stirrup buckles.

Tex didn't even seem to notice the little porker at his feet.

With an indulgent smile, Charlotte had to admit that, just as Tex was not the same man, Toto was not the same pig. As much as she was loath to confess it, the lessons had worked wonders. These days, the little oinker trotted obediently at her heel, never once stopping to root or fling dirt.

Tex nudged the pig off his feet and Toto came to sit upon her sandals. Seemed he had a thing about not sitting in the dirt. She reached down and gave him a pat and murmured some praise, and he rubbed against her leg, encouraging her to continue. A low giggle rumbled from deep in her throat. Really, he was a dear old thing, when he wanted to be.

"Looks like you got a buddy."

"He's all right."

"He's sweet on you."

"How can you tell?"

"I recognize the signs."

She glanced up in time to see Tex smiling at her and felt the heat that shimmered off the ground radiate up into her cheeks. He'd been watching her with Toto and was no doubt getting the erroneous idea that she was becoming an animal person. Oh, Toto was tolerable in his funny little way, and even kind of cute, for a pig. But would she ever run out and buy another pig for a pet? No. Highly unlikely. She knew that she should probably tell Tex not to give her any brownie points for converting to his camp. She was Toto's master by default. Not by choice.

Charlotte couldn't and wouldn't fake something she didn't feel. Not even for a wonderful man like Tex. Not even knowing how it would please him to know that she no longer despised Toto and even thought Kitty was all right. She glanced down at the pup that lay in her arms. Okay, adorable.

But still, it simply wasn't enough.

When and if Tex ever settled down, she knew he'd want a woman with whom could share his dream. His love for animals. As much as she'd come along in her tolerance for four-legged creatures, she was not—Charlotte swallowed against the sudden burning sensation that stung the back of her throat and had her eyes watering—she was not right for Tex.

His whole life was animals. She knew nothing about animals. Unless she counted Toto. And Daisy Mae. And now Kitty. But still, she had to get it through her head that they were from different worlds. In the long run, overlooking these important contrasts would only lead to a heartache.

An animal behaviorist and a...a...what? Charlotte sighed, her shoulders bobbing with silent, mirthless laughter. If she didn't have a clue who or what she was, how could she know what she wanted?

Right now, there was only one thing that Charlotte knew for sure.

She needed her freedom.

Her space.

She needed to take time to discover herself. To strike out and make it on her own. Before she committed to another living soul, she needed to prove that she was capable of taking care of herself. It was time to find another job, and an apartment in Hidden Valley.

"Ready?" Tex's sexy baritone drew her from her reverie as he opened the gate to the paddock and urged his mount to follow him over to where she stood.

"Where's your horse?" If he expected her to ride this monster all by herself, he had another think coming.

"Right here." He nodded at the horse as he stepped back to close the gate.

"Oh. Where's mine?"

"Right here. We're riding double."

''We are?'' Oh, now that was an interesting idea. Suddenly, the ride did not seem nearly as terrifying.

Lazily, he swung into the saddle and, leather creaking, leaned down toward her and extended his arms. ''C'mon.''

''Me? Now?''

He nodded. ''Now's as good a time as any.''

Before she could protest, she found herself lifted into the air and seated in the narrow space betwixt the saddle horn and Tex's sinewy thighs. The top of her head rested just under his chin and the shadow of his beard made a pleasant rasping sound against her hair as he adjusted their positions. His muscular arms held her and the puppy securely in place against a chest rock-solid from life on a ranch. Charlotte was having trouble breathing. Even so, she detected the musky scent of his expensive aftershave, and his minty breath as it tickled her ear.

''C'mon, pig,'' he called and reigned his mount around.

Toto trotted after them as Tex urged the horse away from the paddock fence and out toward the open road. Her heart leaping into her throat, Charlotte looked around from the considerable height.

Why...why...this was...this was...

Magnificent.

A grin started at her lips and engulfed her entire body.

This beast was truly *magnificent!* Why had she never before noticed the astounding, remarkable, exceptional, completely stupefying magnificence of a horse?

The man who handled the giant creature with such ease was equally impressive. Secure in Tex's masculine embrace, she chanced a peek around.

She could see so far.

The ride was so smooth.

Tex's shoulders were so broad. So comfortable.

This was so *wonderful!*

Her heart beating nearly as loudly as the clip-clopping of the horse's hooves, Charlotte was shocked to realize that she was having a ball.

Chapter Eight

Giddy with delight, Charlotte leaned back against Tex and peered up at his handsome profile. As he angled his face toward her, that impudent grin she feared she was falling in love with, bloomed. The mere span of a butterfly's wing separated their lips and she had to fight the desperate urge to run her hand up the back of his neck and pull his head down to bring their lips together. To kiss him until her body went limp in his arms.

She was contemplating the best way to accomplish this tactical maneuver—considering the puppy in her arms—when he glanced back to the horizon, saving her from making a fool of herself yet again.

What was it about this man that made her want to beg him to love her? To make a commitment? To father the children she wasn't even sure she wanted? To throw away her chance at the delicious freedom that had beckoned for so very, very long?

She blinked and tore her eyes away from his face to focus instead on the corded muscles of the forearms that held her in place. Strong arms. With biceps and triceps that strained against the sleeves of his T-shirt. Arms that made her feel small and safe and feminine. Her gaze traveled to his hands, work roughened, and tan. The kind of hands that...

Dang it! What the heck was wrong with her?

Charlotte exhaled noisily and rolled her eyes. What a soft-brained mush-ball she was becoming. She straightened her spine. She had to remain strong. Yes. Impervious to his allure. To this yearning for something that threatened to upset her well-laid plans.

For ten long years, as she had nursed Nanna Dorothy, Charlotte dreamed of living on her own.

Of doing things her own way.

Answering to no one.

Coming and going as she pleased.

But if that's what she wanted, why was she miserable every minute that she spent away from the bossy, arrogant Tex? When they were apart, she longed for his touch. His warm laugh. His quick smile. His kiss. The way his eyes darkened possessively, when he looked at her, smoldering with the as yet unspoken connection that shimmered between them. And yes—she thought back to their first meeting—even his macho, caveman way of commanding a situation had a certain base appeal.

She squirmed against the feelings of physical and emotional excitement that sitting so close to him elicited. She was here to relax. To forget her cares. With a concerted effort, she marshaled her thoughts away from the way the heat dampened and melded their bodies together, making it difficult to tell where he started and she left off. The way his body—

Aauugghh. She heaved an inward groan.

There she went *again*.

Charlotte yanked herself away from Tex's snug embrace and made a great show of leaning over the horse and checking on Toto. Yep. There he was, bouncing happily along behind them, oblivious to the dust that swirled from beneath the horse's hooves and into his now-black snout.

Still craning over the pommel, her gaze shifted from the pig to the grand and changing view that rolled out beyond the road. She drank in the sights as Tex brought them through the back sections of the ranch to where he lived in one of his uncle's bunkhouses built for ranch hands. The Brubaker land was truly spectacular. She was beginning to understand its draw for men who loved the great outdoors. Slowly, she settled back against Tex, reveling in the feel of his rugged body wrapped around her softer one.

All too soon they rounded a curve and dipped into a delightful, shady little gully. Emotions of relief and disappointment warred within Charlotte's heart as the ride came to an end, with disappointment winning by a nose. Riding horseback with Tex was an experience she would not soon forget.

With great interest, her gaze darted hither and yon, taking in the picturesque setting. Before her, clustered together under a thick stand of willows and live oaks, a grouping of rustic cabins sat at the edge of an immense pond. Situated in the center of this backwoods neighborhood for cowboys, the water reflected a deep, sea-blue summer sky through which cottony clouds silently floated over Tex's family ranch.

It was heaven.

"So this is where you live."

"Yep." Tex reined to a stop in front of one of the cabins, swung his leg over the horse's rump and dismounted. "This is the little bunkhouse I share with Kenny." He reached up for her and Charlotte allowed herself, and the puppy she cradled, to fall into his arms.

"It's charming," she murmured, afraid to look up into his face for fear of revealing her feelings. His hands lingered just a tad longer than necessary before he let her go.

"I like it. It's simple. A real change of pace from the way most of us grew up, what with maid service and all."

Charlotte nodded. "I'll say." Beyond the cabins, off in the distance, a slight breeze rippled through vast oceans of grain. Lazily slapping at flies with their tails, herds of longhorn cattle slowly grazed from shade tree to shade tree. Calves bawled for their mothers who lowed in return.

Surprisingly, she found these sounds very peaceful. She closed her eyes for a moment and breathed in the warm, summer air.

Tex plucked a straw from a tuft of grass and poked it between his lips and chewed. "Last night I had Big Daddy's cook make us a lunch, on the off chance that you might want to take a break." He gestured across the road to the dock that floated on the surface of the nearly lake-sized pond. "Why don't you take the animals over there and make yourself comfortable on those lounge chairs under the umbrella? I'll be back in a minute with lunch."

"Okay."

Charlotte set the squirming golden retriever on the ground and tail wagging, Kitty hopped about, feeling frisky. Too frisky. It seemed that the horse did not take kindly to being bitten about the ankles and lashed out with a lightning hoof.

Somersaulting in a cloud of dust, the small dog shrieked in pain, more from a wounded ego than anything, but Charlotte was outraged. "You big, fat tube of glue, what do you think you're doing? Pick on someone your own size," she shouted, her face blazing as she shouldered the half-ton beast off to the side and snatched the howling pup off the ground. "Look what you've done to Kitty. Gave her an owie on her paw. Say you're sorry you big...*boob!*"

The horse's ears twitched and his head slowly swung back to find out what all the commotion was about, back at his tail.

"Are you all right, little sweetie?" Charlotte kissed Kitty's paw and nuzzled her fuzzy head. "That big bully scare you? Poor baby. Next time, you stay away from that big meanie and you won't get hurt." With a huff, she flung her hair out of her face and gave the horse an evil eye that didn't seem to faze him in the least.

Eyes cast down, lips pinched between his fingers, Tex spoke to Charlotte out of the corner of his mouth and struggled to keep the laughter that welled in his throat out of his voice. "Anything else I can get for you while I'm inside?"

Charlotte shifted the now pacified pup down to her feet and thought for a moment. "Do you get the *Hidden Valley Tribune Appeal?*"

He nodded. "Yep. Anything else?"

"A red pencil. Oh and—" she began to unbutton her camp shirt and though Tex knew she was wearing a swimsuit under there, the languid action still played havoc with his senses "—and a cell phone. And a pad of paper..."

"Charlotte, this is our day off."

She smiled that Mona Lisa smile that had his blood

running hot and made him wonder what she was up to. "I know."

"Okay. Anything else?"

"That ought to get me started."

Tex only hoped he could remember her requests. He hadn't really been listening, but instead was focused on her fingers as they moved from button to button. Mesmerized, he walked backward, until he stumbled over Toto and nearly ended up on the ground. "Uh, oops!" His grin was sheepish as he nodded toward the house. "I'll be right back."

He turned and bolted.

Tex couldn't get over how good Charlotte looked in that skimpy black swimsuit of hers as they reclined in the sunshine out at the end of the dock. It was one piece, but it was cut to show off her assets to their best advantage. And Charlotte had assets galore.

He swallowed, forcing his body's reactions to her to chill.

She reclined on her side, long, slender legs pulled up for balance, her top leg dangling over the edge of her lounger. Pale peach toenails curled in Kitty's ruff as she lolled in a patch of shade next to her chair. A ghost of a smile tugged at Tex's mouth. The dog had bonded with her. Followed her everywhere. She may not realize it, but she'd be hard-pressed to get rid of Kitty now.

He peered at her from behind the safety of his sunglasses and he was reasonably sure she thought he was dozing. That was okay. For a few more minutes he just wanted to memorize the way the fantastic curves of her legs flowed into the curves of her hips, then dipping at the curve of her waist and swelling again at the curve of her breast. From these last weeks spent poolside, she'd tanned a light golden brown and her honey-brown mop of curls fairly sparkled with highlights.

Tex exhaled long and slow. If the ride over here hadn't been torture, then this sure as heck was. Several times on the way over, he'd been tempted to throw caution to the wind and kiss her senseless. But he couldn't do that. She wanted her independence. Getting in over his head with Charlotte would be...hell, he was already in over his head. He was staring at a broken heart head-on as it was, especially if she up and decided to get a job and move away.

His mouth went dry as he watched her apply a coat of suntan lotion, first to herself, and then to the pig who sprawled out on a beach towel in the lounger on her other side.

She didn't seem too concerned that *he* might burn, he noted.

Maybe he oughta suggest she dab some of that stuff on his shoulders. And arms. And chest. His breathing became shallow and blinking hard, he adjusted his sunglasses and ordered himself to look out over the pond and watch for jumping catfish.

There were none.

The newspaper crinkled, drawing his attention away from the uncooperative fish. She was at it again. Circling the want ads, looking for employment. The tip of her tongue teased her lower lip and her brow puckered in concentration as she searched.

She seemed to be having no luck and then, a smile of triumph lit her face.

His heart sank. Another job. Third time had to be the charm. If she was successful, she'd move away. She'd been yammering about getting out there on her own for days. What was so glamorous about living by herself was beyond him. Grumpily, he smacked at a mosquito. She seemed to want her solitude. Her damned independence.

"Find something?" he inquired, hoping not.

"Mmm, mmm, mmm." She sat up, her body fairly vibrating with anticipation.

"That good?"

"Um-hum."

"What's it going to be this time? Hair stuff? Nail junk?"

"Nope. I'm done with the fashion world, remember?" Beaming, she pointed at the section she'd circled. "ReadyMaid home care products. I have a good feeling about this one."

"Never heard of 'em."

"They're new."

"More home parties?"

"Well, yes, but this is different. I just know it. Everyone has to clean their house. And these products sound wonderful. I'll put on a show for the staff. Miss Clarise can call her friends and they can send their staff…"

As she scribbled on her pad, her eyes snapped and sparkled with ideas.

"Need any help?"

She drew her lower lip between her teeth and considered his offer for a long while before she finally nodded. "Yes."

"Need me to assist at the party?"

"Sure, that would be great. And," she swallowed, "if you don't mind, in the next few days, when you have some free time, I'd like you to help me hunt for an apartment."

Tex reached to his throat to monitor his pulse. *An apartment?* Doggone it. She wasn't fooling around this time.

"If I land this job, I'm going to get serious about moving out. I've depended on the kindness of relatives for far too long. It's time to strike out on my own."

"Okay." Tex sighed.

"Can I use your cell phone? I'm gonna call ReadyMaid and see when I can get started. Then I'll call Miss Clarise and arrange a party, and after that, I'll line up a few apartments to look at this weekend, in my price range."

"Sure."

All the sunshine and glory seemed to eke out of his wonderful, lazy day and the delightful picnic lunch that Cook had prepared suddenly weighed heavily on his gut. Time for a cooling swim, he decided glumly and rolled out of the lounger that sat at the edge of the dock, and into the frigid water.

"So why don't you run the ranch?"

Charlotte leaned back in Tex's arms and peered up at him, causing his heart to bounce around in his rib cage. The sun was low in the evening sky and, drowsy from a day of relaxation and good food, they had packed up their picnic and were headed back to the stables on the horse. The low, sleepy alto of her voice was a melody to his ears.

"Didn't want to. I worked as a ranch hand for several years, but passed the foreman baton to my cousin Kenny when my turn came up."

"Why?"

"Wanted to start up my clinic."

"Why didn't you want to work for your dad?"

"Wanted to work for myself."

"Why do the rest of the guys work on the ranch when

you all could be running big businesses for your fathers?''

He looked down and her and grinned. ''You sure are full of questions.''

''I can't help it.'' Leaning back, she shot him sassy grin of her own. ''You're interesting.''

Time suspended. The horse seemed to suddenly be walking in slow motion. She was so beautiful. The magic light of the evening sun suffused her complexion with a pale, golden glow and kindled a fire in her eyes.

With a heavy sigh, he tightened his grip at her waist and labored to remember her question. Oh, yeah.

''The reason we all take turns working the ranch is that my dad and Big Daddy feel that having us spend some time doing hard labor makes men out of us. And I expect they're right. Big business, much like ranch life, is not for weak men.''

''No,'' she murmured, ''it's not.''

''Usually one of the Brubaker sons or nephews will run Big Daddy's ranch or work as a hand, before taking over one of the family companies, but some have gone into other lines of work. Rogues, I guess.''

''Like you.''

''More like my cousin, Buck. He runs an orphanage, which was the first real departure for our family. His sister, Patsy, and her husband, Justin, work there, too.''

''How come none of the daughters ever get to run the ranch?''

''So far, none of 'em have asked.'' He grinned at her inquisitive nature and wondered if she'd apply for a job, if the cleaning supply thing didn't work out. He doubted it. Too many animals for her taste. ''Although, my sister-in-law, Sydney, worked as a hand for a while, before she married my brother, Montana. But that's another story.''

"I can see why you like it out here."

"Really, why?"

Charlotte lifted her shoulders and gave her head a little shake. Her eyes had a dreamy, distant quality as she looked off into the horizon. "I don't know. It's so big. Spacious. You don't feel hemmed in, the way you do in the suburbs."

"True."

"This must have been a great place to grow up." Her voice took on a wistful quality.

"It was. We lived here in the summers, pretty much, and during the school year when we weren't here, we were nearby on my dad's spread, and Big Daddy's kids were over, hanging out with us. Sometimes, it was like having seventeen brothers and sisters."

"Yikes."

"Yeah, always somebody to fight with."

"Is that why you're so good at fighting now?" She looked back at him, amusement playing on her lips.

"I like to think I'm better at loving these days."

"Oh?"

"Yeah. I had a wonderful time today," he murmured in her ear, and it was true, except for the part about her wanting to move away from the ranch and strike out on her own.

"Me, too." Much to his pleasure, she sounded quite breathless.

"We should play hooky more often."

"Mmm." Her eyes slid closed.

Way before he was ready to be back, the horse had spotted the stable and was picking up speed. Toto made a valiant effort to keep up and all too soon, they were back and their leisurely day was coming to a close. Tex wanted to prolong the minutes with Charlotte, and wracked his brain for a way.

Once they'd dismounted and put the horse away, Tex took Charlotte's hand and they strolled back toward his office.

"I'll make a pot of coffee and we can get the animals fed and cleaned up."

"Okay, but I can't stay long."

"Why not?" He glanced away to hide the sudden wave of disappointment he felt. No doubt he was wearing his heart on his sleeve. Again.

"I have to go feed Daisy Mae and the kids. She's been out there in this heat all day, and I haven't checked on her since early this morning."

"Oh."

Striving to appear nonchalant, he fished for the keys to his office door and was surprised to discover that the door was already open. What the—? After hours, the door was always to be locked and the lights turned out.

"Wally?" he called, noting the blazing lights and the sound of his stereo playing.

No answer.

Charlotte stepped into his office after him, her jaw dropping in amazed amusement. "Looks like a bomb went off in here." Her nose wrinkled. "Smells like one, too."

"More chemistry tests. If you think this is bad, you should smell the storeroom." Tex ran his hands over the back of his neck and rotated his head. "I can't believe that guy."

"He is a slob." Charlotte gestured to the chalkboard. "But at least he left you a note."

The words *Out with Mona* had been hastily scrawled

there. The phone was not quite hung up and the cap to his highlighter was still off.

"Looks like he was in a hurry. Must be studying a different kind of chemistry." With a knowing smile Charlotte moved over to Wally's work space and snapped the lid back on his yellow pen.

"The call of the wild."

Charlotte laughed. "You'll have to cut him some slack then."

"Yeah. That's a tough call to ignore."

"Especially on a Saturday night."

"You sure you have to go check up on those goats?"

"Tex Brubaker! I'm surprised at you. Of course I have to feed the goats." She spun on her heel and snapped her fingers for Toto. "What do you take me for? Some kind of moron?" she groused over her shoulder as she marched out of his office and into the evening shadows.

Tex grinned. He wondered how long it would be before she realized that the hapless Kitty still bobbed over her arm.

An hour later, Charlotte pulled up in front of Nanna Dorothy's house, grateful to have escaped Tex's office before she did something really impulsive. Stupid. Something that would thwart her efforts to strike out on her own. Slowly, she unhooked her safety belt, and debated turning around and roaring back to the ranch. To the magnetic pull of Tex's sexy gaze. To his solid, electrifying embrace. To the feel of his mouth on hers.

She blinked and Nanna Dorothy's monstrous abode came into focus. The home where she'd been a virtual prisoner for ten long years. To rid herself of the claustrophobic feelings that suddenly threatened to overwhelm her, she leapt from the car and called for her pig.

Upon entering the old house, she couldn't help but notice the thick, cottony hush that seemed to have settled within. Even with the lights glowing cheerily in the den, even with Toto and Kitty prowling around together in the hall, even knowing that Daisy Mae and her babies were just a driveway away, it still seemed so desolate. Isolated.

And so very lonely.

The chair behind Nanna's old desk creaked as Charlotte sank down and listened to the quiet. This is what it would be like, if she were on her own, she realized. For a long moment, she allowed herself to pretend that she lived by herself, as Nanna Dorothy had for so many years. What would a typical evening entail?

The clock in the front hall chimed the hour. The hours till bedtime seemed to yawn endlessly ahead.

Charlotte looked around the room at the shelves loaded with musty books, yellowed with age. That's what she would do if she had all the time in the world on her hands. She would indulge in the luxury of reading. Why, she could read every book in this den, if she pleased. She could stay up all blasted night reading. Unless, of course, she had to work the next day. And when she was done reading? Well, she could sew. Okay, that wasn't exactly true, but she could certainly learn to sew. And play the piano, and knit, and do little craft projects and putter in the kitchen and watch TV, and gosh, the list seemed endless.

Endlessly dull.

Charlotte settled back and continued to listen. She listened to the steady thud of her heartbeat. To the sad, haunting silence. To the dreary existence she would lead, sequestered away from the rest of the world, because she had something to prove. The image of herself at Nanna

Dorothy's age, surrounded by yards of yarn crafts as she banged away at the piano, filled her mind.

Her eyes slid closed and she grew very still as her thoughts changed direction.

All of these things that she thought she wanted... Couldn't she do them if she were married?

And had children?

And maybe a pig and a dog or two?

But that wasn't part of the plan, she reminded herself. Was it?

Restless, Charlotte stood, shook off the funk that had taken hold and began loading the bag of paperwork that she'd abandoned last week when Daisy Mae had been in trouble. Remembering the folder in the safe, she entered the combination and pulled out the envelope containing the video and tossed it into the bag. She could go over that stuff back home, at the Brubakers' place. The entertainment center in her suite's parlor had a TV and a VCR.

She was gathering food and water for Daisy Mae when the sound of a door slamming filtered through the kitchen window. Sounded like it came from the Martkowski place. Charlotte tiptoed over to the sink and pushed the curtains back. There was a light on next door. The Martkowskis were home.

The outrage that she'd been nursing for a week now, surged to the forefront as she marched over to their front stoop and leaned on their doorbell. Through the sidelight, Charlotte could see the nerves in Mrs. Martkowski's expression as she peeked outside into the shadows. The porch light came on and the safety chain rattled.

"Yes? What is it?" Mrs. Martkowski inquired. "Oh, Charlotte! I didn't expect to see you here." She fumbled with the locks and finally had the door open. "Hello, dear. Gracious, I'm so sorry about your great-grandmother. I know I haven't had time to come by and—"

"Right." Charlotte waved an impatient hand and tossed her hair out of her face to better eyeball her neighbor. "Listen, Mrs. Martkowski, I just want to tell you that I don't appreciate you leaving Daisy Mae, pregnant with twins, no less, out in this horrendous heat to die. An animal cannot be expected to live without food or water for an entire—"

"I...I...wha...?" Mrs. Martkowski's mouth gaped. "No food? No water? But we hired a service!"

"You did?" Some of the wind in Charlotte's sails died.

"Yes. A pet-sitting service. For the entire week."

"They never showed up. I know. I have taken care of Daisy Mae and her babies several times a day the whole time you were gone."

"Why, that's impossible! I paid in advance." Mrs. Martkowski looked truly mortified. "Charlotte, please, come inside for a moment, won't you?"

Charlotte waited in the entry hall, while Mrs. Martkowski made a phone call and then conferred with her equally horrified husband. When she returned, she was all at once grateful and disgusted. "They had us down for next week. Charlotte, I'm so very sorry. I can't begin to thank you enough. Daisy Mae means the world to Herb and me! She's the one thing we kept after we sold Granddad's farm and if anything ever happened to her, well—" tears brimmed in the woman's eyes as she reached for her purse and began to rummage around. "I want to give you a reward for your time and heroism."

"No, no. Mrs. Martkowski, that's really not necessary. Anybody would have done the same."

"That's simply not true, my dear. In this day and age,

finding someone who cares the way you do, especially about a simple farm animal, is a rarity indeed. Your Nanna Dorothy was a wonderful friend to me for all the years we were neighbors. I really feel as if I must give you a reward.''

Charlotte didn't want to insult the poor woman. Especially since she seemed so distraught. But still, she did not take care of the Martkowski goat in hopes of receiving a reward. She did it because she couldn't stand to see the dumb goat suffer. "Really, I—"

"Please."

Charlotte sagged. "If you insist."

Mrs. Martkowski withdrew a set of keys from her purse and led Charlotte through the house to the backyard. "Pick one of Daisy Mae's babies for your own, honey. I promise you, a goat will give you years of pleasure and fine company.''

Chapter Nine

"Whatcha got there?"

"What's it look like?" Charlotte groused as she struggled through his office door, towing a bona fide menagerie behind her.

Tex raised a brow. She seemed distinctly grumpy this fine Monday morning. He peered over his desk. "A goat."

"No—" sarcasm dripped "—it's my *reward*. For taking care of Daisy Mae when the pet-sitting service screwed up. Meet Ozzie."

"Ozzie?"

"As in the Wizard of? Nanna Dorothy would have loved it." Charlotte shouted over her shoulder. "Daisy Mae!" To Tex she explained, "Apparently Ozzie is too young to move away from his mommy and sister so Mrs. Martkowski insisted I take them until they are weaned. Isn't that great?"

Daisy Mae and her other baby trotted into Tex's office and stood surveying their surroundings.

Tex threw back his head and howled at the pained expression on her face. This was just so perfect. Before long, she'd be the owner of a veritable zoo. He hiked his boots up onto his desktop and settled back to laugh himself sick.

With a disgusted snort, Charlotte slammed the office door, let go of the various leashes she held and staggered to the coffeepot. Her hair was not arranged into its usual tidy coif, and her clothes were distinctly wrinkled. She turned to stare at him. Obviously, she did not see the humor of the situation quite the way he did.

"Can we skip the lesson thing this morning?"

Tex wiped his eyes. "Sure, I guess so. But I have to leave town tomorrow morning for an overnight conference in Houston, so we're going to be skipping three days in a row."

She grew very still. "You're going to be gone? Overnight?"

"Yeah. Why? You gonna miss me?"

Flustered and slightly hot in the cheeks, she ignored his impertinent question. "That's okay," she said, "we can pick up where we left off when you get back."

"Fine. So what's up?"

"I got a phone call from the ReadyMaid company earlier today. I'm in. Their local rep is delivering my starter kit this afternoon, and I've already talked to Miss Clarise. We are holding our first party tonight."

"Tonight? Why so soon?"

"No time like the present."

"Okay." He sobered slightly, "Why does that interfere with our lesson?"

"I want you to take me apartment hunting in Hidden Valley this morning. I've got an offer on Nanna Dorothy's house, so I'm going to need a place to put some of my furniture. Plus, now that I have a job, I don't have any more excuses to sponge off Miss Clarise and Big Daddy. Maybe if I commit to an apartment, I'll have to make a go of the job this time.'' Her smile didn't quite reach her eyes.

Suddenly, Tex was no longer laughing. He swung his feet off his desk top and, propping his elbows on his blotter, gazed up at her beautiful face. ''So you're serious about this living alone thing.''

Uncertainty flashed across her features and was then replaced by determination. ''Yes.'' Eyes narrowed to sapphire slits, delicate jaw set, she inhaled deeply through her teeth, seeming to steel herself against any objection he might have. ''I have a list of places to look at that take pets, and I've made some phone calls, so please, go with me. I don't want to go alone.''

''Why not?''

She shrugged. ''I don't know. I just don't. I've never done this kind of thing before.''

He grunted.

''Is that a yes?''

He nodded.

''Then we can go with you whenever you're ready.''

''We?''

''I have to take the pig and the goats,'' she said so matter-of-factly it sounded as if she were referring to her children.

''Right.'' Tex turned so that she couldn't see him smile. Maybe there was hope for her after all. ''I'll bring the Jeep around,'' he called over his shoulder.

''You can't stay here.''

Charlotte looked askance at Tex and saw the muscles twitching in his jaw.

"Why not?" If her tone was belligerent, it's because he'd said that about every place they'd seen that morning. She was beginning to regret bringing him along. She'd thought he might be helpful in the decision-making process, but he was becoming a royal pain in the butt.

This building, albeit run-down, was the pick of the litter. At least this place accepted pets. All kinds, according to the building superintendent. Charlotte couldn't be sure, but it sounded like the neighbors had a horse.

"Because it's a dump, that's why." His eyes glittered with irritation.

"So what? It's temporary and it's mine."

"Not yet, it's not."

"It will be, as soon as I sign on the dotted line," she hissed. She lowered her voice even further so that the less-than-super super couldn't overhear their private conversation. Their bowed heads and hushed whispers hadn't seemed to put him off yet. The very strange, very nosy man hovered just outside the unit, watching their every move and all but pressing a glass to the wall.

She and Tex stepped from the minuscule foyer and moved farther into the living room area, which had clearly seen more than its share of living. The plaster was falling off the walls in chunks, exposing the pipes and wires beneath. Dark brown water and nicotine stains formed dirty patterns on the ceiling and Charlotte didn't even want to think about what the spots on the ancient shag carpeting were from. Especially considering the way they seemed to fascinate the animals. But it was within her price range so who was she to quibble?

Ominous thunderclouds brewed over Tex's head. Arms folded across his chest, legs spread for balance, he looked down at her, his usually present dimples in hiding. "No way are you moving in here."

"Shhhh!" Over her shoulder, she smiled brightly out the door at the derelict superintendent and then whipped her head back to Tex. "He might hear you."

"Hey, buddy, she's not moving into this dump," Tex called.

"We haven't decided yet," Charlotte called after Tex. The super pressed his face to the screen door.

Charlotte whapped Tex on the arm then pulled his ear to her mouth. "Would you knock it off? I can't afford anything else on my salary!"

"What salary?"

"I'll be making some money. Soon." She tossed another wide smile back at the snoopy super. "Listen, Tex. Since the day we met, you've been hinting about me moving out. Well, the moment has arrived, and you're stalling. What's the matter with you?"

"What's the matter with *me?*" His hand snaked out and gripping her arm, he yanked her to his side.

She gave a little yelp of surprise.

"Hey, buddy, excuse us for a minute, will ya?" Tex took a step back and with the heel of his boot, kicked at the front door.

"I...uh...okay," the super simpered.

With a bang, the door slammed in his peering face. Tex pushed Charlotte up against the crumbling plaster of the living room wall and closed his hands around her upper arms, effectively locking her in place.

Voice low, eyes sparking, he growled at her, his breath tickling the flyaway hairs at the side of her face. "What do you mean what's the matter with me? What's the matter with *you?* You think I want you to move? Don't go pinning this harebrained scheme on me, sister. I don't want you to move. I've never wanted you to move."

"Never?" she whispered, breathless.

"No," he shouted. "It's all *you've* talked about since you've moved into Big Daddy's place. How you need to move back out again. How you need your damned independence. Your *space.* How you need to prove that you can make it on your own."

"But I've never had any real freedom," she whimpered.

"That is such a crock. Listen to yourself. You are free! This is a free country, Charlotte Beauchamp. Come and go as you please, nobody's stopping you, least of all me. But I will tell you one thing. If you think that I—or any other member of my family for that matter—will let you move into this place by yourself, you're crazy."

Charlotte was sure her heart was skipping some very important beats. She hoped Tex, or that guy who was staring at them through the front window knew CPR.

"You wanna know what I think, lady?"

"W-w-what?"

"I think I've given you far too much space," he ground out through his tightly clenched jaw. His eyes stabbed into hers, causing her heart to stop altogether for a moment, before it threatened to beat its way out of her chest. Her breath began to come in ragged little puffs as his mouth closed in on hers. "I think," Tex let go of her arms and with a groan, settled the hard length of his body against hers and buried his hands in her hair. "I think," he muttered against her lips, "that what you need is a little less space."

That said, his mouth claimed hers, and he kissed her hard, with an intensity that swept over them both like a twister ravaging Tornado Alley.

Their kiss grew rapidly urgent. Heated. Charlotte arched into him, sure that she'd finally found what had been missing her entire life. *This was it!* The foggy thought swirled through her head. This yearning. This longing. This ache she'd harbored in her heart all her life for some nebulous excitement that she thought freedom would bring.

But that's not what she really wanted at all.

Loving Tex brought her a whole new kind of freedom.

His breathing as ragged as her own, Tex broke the kiss and let his forehead fall against hers, seemingly to collect his wits. Her head lolled back against the wall and he kissed the exposed flesh at her jawline.

"You're not moving in here," he growled.

"Okay," she breathed.

"You're coming home with me." His lips traveled from her jaw, down her neck, to her collarbone and on to the hollow of her throat.

Charlotte moaned. "Okay."

"You're not going to move at all."

"I'm not going anywhere."

"Good." Cradling her head in his hands, he found her mouth once more, and in this kiss, they gave into all the passion they'd denied since the day they'd met. After a long moment, Tex, breathing hard, pulled back and kissed the tip of her nose. "Very good. Because—" his smile was rueful "—I don't think I'm in any shape to walk out of here, just yet."

Charlotte giggled. "Don't look now, but I think the super's eyes have glazed over."

"Yet another reason why there is no way you're moving in here."

"Why? You planning on kissing me some more?"

"Every chance I get."

That evening, as Charlotte looked out over the standing-room-only crowd in Miss Clarise's parlor, she was eternally grateful for Tex's steadying presence at her side. Perhaps she'd been a bit impulsive, planning her first party for tonight. Inviting quite so many people may have also been a mistake, as she was sure that a great number could neither see, nor hear her from their seats out in the foyer. Obviously, the word had spread. Charlotte Beauchamp might not sell you anything, but the demonstrations were always highly entertaining.

She sighed.

Never mind. She was tired of living in limbo. She wanted a real job, and she wanted it now. She might not care quite so much for her independence since she'd given that some serious rethinking with Tex's generous— she flushed as the memories of his lips on hers came flooding back—help this morning. But she did want to pay her own way in this world.

So far, she and Tex had stumbled through the ReadyMaid introduction and several product demonstrations, that were more or less successful. It was now time to wow 'em with the grand finale. Charlotte took a deep breath and smiled a million watter at the audience.

"EttaMae—" she gestured to the frowsy woman who sat near the foyer arch, a mixed look of fear and suspicion on her face "—if you could now go to the kitchen and bring us the pans that you and the staff used to bake and cook with today, we will demonstrate the WonderKleen pot-scrubber solution."

Tex dug the bottle of WonderKleen out of the case and held it up for all to see.

EttaMae grunted and stood.

"Be sure to bring us your toughest jobs," she sang.

EttaMae pushed her way through the crowd in the foyer and disappeared.

"While we are waiting, Tex and I would like to show

you how to clean those impossible-to-remove stains from your carpet, with WonderKleen for carpets.''

Tex's sisters, sitting in their usual spot on the couch, laughed and catcalled. Hands planted on his narrow hips, he shot them a menacing glance that did nothing more than spur them on.

"Show us how to clean that spot, carpet-boy," Ginny sang.

"Yeah, bay-bee," Mary hooted.

"I gotta take a picture of this for Mom or she'll never believe it." Georgia's camera flashed several times.

Smiling, Charlotte ignored the fracas and carried on. "If you will take this ink, and pour it on Miss Clarise's priceless white carpet, please?"

Tex frowned. "Ink?" With a dubious glance at Miss Clarise, he took the bottle. "Are you sure?"

Miss Clarise nodded her permission.

Charlotte held up the literature and smiled with confidence. "WonderKleen obliterates ink stains and guarantees absolutely no trace of the spillage, or your money back."

Tex hesitated.

"Go on," she urged under her breath, then tossed another self-assured smile at the crowd.

At her bidding, Tex bent down and spilled a good-sized spot of black ink on Miss Clarise's one-of-a-kind white-on-white Turkish rug.

The audience gasped and strained forward attempting to catch a glimpse of this derring-do.

"Now then," Charlotte continued to read from the literature. "Simply rub a teaspoon of WonderKleen solvent into the affected area, and the stain will disappear as if by magic." She handed Tex a spoon.

EttaMae, pots and pans clanking, returned from the

kitchen and fought her way up to the podium. "You said bring 'em dirty," she barked, thrusting her dripping pans at Charlotte, "so I did."

"Uh, er…thank you, EttaMae." Charlotte beamed at the audience. Great globs of marinara sauce plopped to the floor, further staining the fabulous imported rug. "Oops. Well, it's a lucky thing we have plenty of WonderKleen," she noted as Tex worked a teaspoon of the solvent into the ink stain.

EttaMae frowned. "Say. Is it supposed to smoke like that?"

Tex jumped to his feet and they all three bent to stare at the odd phenomena. Sure enough, EttaMae was right. Little puffs of smoke spewed forth from the carpet, then turned into bigger puffs and were soon beginning to swirl from the stain and into the air.

"Looks like it's eatin' a hole clean through the danged carpet," EttaMae declared. "So that's how it works!" She looked up at Charlotte. "Ya ain't gonna get your money back. Like the flyer says, the stain is gone."

The audience gasped.

EttaMae coughed a reedy, rattling cough. "That stuff is strong. Kinda burns the nose." Eyes watering and bulging, she continued to hack.

Charlotte looked to Tex with concern. EttaMae seemed to be choking. She patted the older woman on the back and handed her the glass of water she kept under the podium.

The steamy smoke that sizzled from the carpet did have a rather pungent, almost toxic smell. Growing worried, Charlotte joined Tex in trying to stamp out what appeared to be a fireless fire with their shoes. When that didn't work, she grabbed the water glass from the sputtering EttaMae and poured it on the rug.

Ever graceful, Miss Clarise announced an intermission to be held in the rose garden. They would return, she promised, after Poison Control had been there to filter the air.

"I wish you didn't have to leave."

"I do, too." Tex had just loaded the last of his luggage, briefcase, computer and PowerPoint presentation Wally had prepared, into his Jeep. With a brave smile, he turned and drew her into his arms. "But it's just for one night. I'll be back tomorrow afternoon."

It was the morning after their first ReadyMaid party. Though it had been an unmitigated disaster, Charlotte felt closer to Tex than ever before. As usual, he'd been wonderful and understanding and so very supportive. How she'd managed to live for so many years without him, boggled her mind. And now, just as they were discovering each other, he had to leave town to speak at an Animal Research Institute conference in Houston. Though it was only to be for a day, it would surely feel like forever.

The feel of his arms around her was bliss. Why had she fought this heaven on earth for so long? She sighed heavily. Because she'd been confused. Naive. Well, no longer. She couldn't wait till Tex got back, and they could spend some quality time really getting to know each other on a more intimate basis.

She rested her cheek against the soft fabric of his shirt and listened to the steady thrumming of his heart. He leaned back just a fraction and tipped her chin up.

"Hurry back?" she whispered.

With a nod, he lowered his lips to hers for a quick, light kiss that was just meant to whet her appetite. "Yes." He nibbled her lower lip.

"Mmm. Drive carefully."

"Always."

"You'll call?"

He patted the cell phone that he'd tucked in her pocket. "You'll hold the fort down?"

"I suppose I should, since I own at least half of the animals in there."

He chuckled. "Keep an eye on Wally."

"Do I have to?"

"Just don't fall for his sustained eye-contact seduction."

Charlotte pulled a face. "Not much chance of that."

"Good." Again, Tex kissed Charlotte for all he was worth, and then tore his mouth from hers and stood there, breathing like a locomotive. "I gotta go."

The phone rang and Charlotte shouted at her menagerie to get out from under her feet as she stumbled from her bedroom and into her parlor. Diving over the couch, she landed with a thud, snatched up the phone and greeted the caller with breathless anticipation.

"Hello?"

"Charlotte?"

It was Tex. Two hours had passed since he'd left and they'd been the loneliest of her life. She tried to inject a note of serenity into her voice, but it was impossible, given the thrill she felt at the sound of his husky voice.

"Tex! What's going on?"

"Well, I just checked into the hotel room and I'm supposed to be reviewing Wally's research for my presentation, but I decided that I'd rather talk to you."

"I rank over sustained eye contact?"

"Hard to believe, isn't it?"

The trio of goats circled the coffee table, looking for

food and a way to climb up. "Go lie down!" Charlotte instructed, waving her arms and pointing.

"I love it when you're bossy."

"Not you. The Animal Farm. They're all here. Toto says he misses you."

"You've got five animals in your suite with you?"

Charlotte sighed and sang. "Everywhere that Charlotte went, the gang was sure to go."

"At least you're not lonely."

"Am, too." She pulled Kitty into her lap and scratched his tummy. "What are you going to do now?"

"Register for the conference, have lunch, network, and then come back here and go over all the stuff Wally loaded into my briefcase for the presentation tomorrow. This is his one chance to redeem himself. If he blows this, he's fired for sure."

"You can't cut him just a little slack? He's in love, you know."

"Yeah, well, I'm in love and I don't go around acting like a dork."

Charlotte froze, not knowing how to respond to his reference to love. Luckily he didn't seem to require one, and kept on talking.

"What are you going to do all day?"

She cleared her throat and tried to think past the racket her heart was making. "Oh, I'll probably read some more of those manuals on training the seeing-eye dog. Maybe I'll try to get Kitty to sit and stay. She's going to make some lucky person a wonderful service dog. Nanna Dorothy would have loved having a seeing-eye dog, I think. I don't suppose Toto could have been trained for such purposes?"

Tex chuckled. "A seeing-eye pig? Nope. Would never work. Pigs have different brains."

"Toto's smart," she defended.

Tex laughed. "Don't deny that you're getting sweet on that pig."

"I am not."

"So you're spending the entire day working with animals?"

"Mainly. But first I thought I'd watch this video I found in Nanna Dorothy's safe, and go over some of the papers that go with that, and then I'm gonna go feed the animals and check on Wally when he gets in."

"He's supposed to be there all night tonight. Don't let him sneak out to party with Mona. And keep the clinic doors and all the kennels locked. People come in and out of the Circle BO all the time. Some of those dogs are priceless."

"Roger, boss."

"Charlotte?"

"Hmm?"

"I really, really miss you."

"Me, too," she whispered. "Me, too."

An hour later, Charlotte still sat upon the comfortable couch in the parlor area of her suite at the Brubaker mansion, the remote control to the VCR dangling from her fingertips in one hand, the other hand absently scratching Toto's head. The papers from the envelope that had contained the video from Nanna Dorothy's safe were spread out before her on the coffee table.

"Well, I'll be doggoned," she murmured, as the image of Nanna Dorothy's smiling face faded to black. When the tape hit the end, the VCR clicked into rewind mode and began to hum. The television hissed with the static snow that danced upon the now blank screen.

On the mantle, the clock ticked away the minutes and

Charlotte stared into space and pondered her great-grandmother's final words. Good old Nanna Dorothy was full of wee-wee and vinegar till the very end it seemed.

Suddenly, the humor of the situation hit Charlotte and she leaned back in against the plush throw pillows and howled with laughter.

Chapter Ten

Wally was gone.

Typical, Charlotte thought, pushing through the unlocked door into Tex's brightly lit office that evening. She'd left Kitty in her room and Ozzie and his family grazing in a small pen on the other side of the stables. Toto, however, stumbled and gamboled in upon her heels. From the sound of the dogs that barked back in the kennel, Wally had neglected to feed them before he'd taken off.

Once again, Wally had left a cryptic note to his whereabouts on the chalkboard. *Out to dinner with Mona, back soon, Wally.*

"Glad you thought to fill your own belly first," Charlotte grumbled, and searched for the keys to the kennel among the rat's nest that was Wally's study area. After a quarter hour's search, she finally located the keys and made her first stop the kennel which was filled with jumping, yapping and very hungry dogs. "Hold on to your hats, ladies and gentlemen, mama's-a-comin'."

She had to lug the fifty pound bag of dog food behind her, because Wally had forgotten to fill the bins. "Wally, my boy, you are so fired. Cuz if Tex don't fire ya, I will." Mumbling all the while, she set out the dog food, filled their water dishes, and stopped to console the more excitable dogs. "Hey, Rex, old boy, how you doin'? Come here, buddy. You don't say? Well, I give you permission to bite the weird guy when he comes back. But only after me, okay? Good boy. That's a sweetie. Oh, such kisses. Yesssss. Okay, I'll let all you guys out to play in a minute. Eat now, while I clean up uncle Tex's office, okay?"

After about an hour, Charlotte had the dogs fed, exercised and put away for the night. She'd cleaned up the sink in the kitchenette, washed the coffee cups and wiped down the counter. Then she set to straightening Tex's desk. Sitting in his chair and touching his things almost made her feel as if he were there. As she'd seen him do a hundred times before, she leaned back, springs and leather creaking and squeaking and put her feet up on the newly organized desktop. Perhaps she would just close her eyes for a moment while she waited for Wally to return.

After all, she thought, taking a deep breath and listening to her pig settle down under her chair, it was lonely back in her suite. She hated being lonely. Here, she felt closer to her sweet Tex. Also, the second Wally came back, she was well and truly going to bite his head off.

Toto was squealing and ramming her chair with his head. Charlotte roused long enough to bat at him and try to return to the lovely dream she was having about Tex holding her and kissing her… *Ahhh.* Fireworks bursting into the air, cracking and popping.

Toto continued with his annoying interruptions.

"Toto, shut up!" she muttered and wriggled around in Tex's big desk chair, looking for a more comfortable position.

"Reeeet!" Toto screamed and plunged his snout through the arm rest and into her thigh.

"Toto, I mean it. If you don't shut up, I'm gonna throw you on the griddle for sure. With two eggs, sunny side…" Charlotte's eyes drifted open. What was that smell?

She sat up, sniffing. Something was not right.

"Reet! Reeeeeet!" Toto screeched, and ran, like a veritable Lassie, to the door that led to the back storeroom. *"Reeeet!"*

"Okay, boy, I'm coming."

Rubbing her eyes, Charlotte pushed back from Tex's desk and stood. It was then that she noticed the smoke pouring from under the door. Fire?

The repeated scream of a security siren suddenly rent the quiet.

Fire! The animal clinic was on fire!

Out the window, she could see flames shooting from the roof over the storeroom, and reaching toward the sky. Looked like the whole back end of the clinic was engulfed in flames already. When had all this happened? She'd been asleep. Tex's beloved animal clinic was burning, and she'd been just lying there.

Charlotte rushed to the door that led to the back storeroom, and laid her fingers against its surface with a tentative touch. *Hot.* Scalding hot. She jerked her hand back, sucked her fingers and wracked her brain to remember the safety films she'd seen on the subject. Under no circumstance, should she open that door, that much she knew. Something about a backdraft and…kaboom.

Get the animals, a voice in her brain instructed.

"Right. The animals. The animals. The animals." All the dogs were locked in the kennel. Where were the keys? What had she done with the blasted keys? She had them just a little while ago, she knew, because she'd had to search...and search. What the hell had she done with the keys?

Something exploded and Charlotte could hear glass shattering. An involuntary scream welled into her throat.

This place was a bomb waiting to go off. Deciding to forego the keys, she ran back to the kennel, Toto following. As if sensing the danger, the dogs were going crazy, yapping and barking so that Charlotte could barely hear herself think. At the first pen, she rattled a chain link door and the dog within stretched up on its hind feet and attempted to lick her face.

"Hang on, sweetie, I'll get you out."

Smoke, coming from Tex's office, was now filling the kennel. Time was running out. Dropping to her knees, she crawled to the end of the hall and found a metal stool used in grooming. She grabbed hold of its legs, and with a brute strength born of fear, one at a time, bashed in the chain-link gates, just enough for her to pull the animal through and set it free.

Barking, licking, wagging, the dogs bounded out of the kennel and back into Tex's office. The door to the back room was gone and flames were now devouring Wally's paperwork and the pie-safe full of books. In the back, more glass shattered. Rafters crashed to the floor. The temperature in the office was suddenly as hot as Hades on a midsummer day. Still down on the floor, Charlotte felt in front of her for the exit, which she supposed to be in front of her.

But it wasn't.

She was lost.

"Charlotte?"

Off in the distance, it sounded like Tex's voice shouting her name. But that couldn't be. Tex was in Houston. She must be losing her faculties.

"Charlotte? Charlotte, sweetheart! Answer me!"

"Tex?" she croaked, wondering if the bright light she saw was part of the fire or part of her heavenly reward.

"Charlotte? Toto?"

"Tex!" Charlotte's paper-thin scream was barely audible above the din. Where was the blasted door? Her heart pounded so high in her throat she feared she'd choke. Loud snuffling sounds let her know the pig was nearby and he pranced excitedly, seeming to respond to the voice that called from beyond.

"Toto?" Charlotte coughed.

Toto nudged her, his damp snout pressed to her ear. Feeling increasingly weak and disoriented from smoke inhalation, she grabbed onto his collar and held on for dear life. They scraped and dragged along the floor until finally he found the front door. Charlotte fell coughing and sputtering out into the night, the dogs pouring out behind her.

Immediately, strong arms surrounded her and lifted her to her feet, guiding her away from the burning building. Charlotte squinted through the smoke to find that it was Tex who held her so tightly.

"Oh, Tex," she blubbered and sagged into his comforting embrace, "thank God you're here!" Rearing back, she stared at him, still not quite sure she could believe her eyes. "What are you doing here? You're supposed to be in Houston!"

"I decided to come back."

In the distance, she could hear the familiar shouts of the ranch hands, as they ran down the road toward the clinic to battle the blaze. Charlotte was barely aware of the siren still throbbing at air-raid force in the clinic as she gulped in great lungfuls of fresh, smoke-free air.

Big Daddy, Fuzzy, Red, Hunt and Colt came rushing up just in time to see Tex leading Charlotte away from the porch. Big Daddy hollered into his cell phone and soon the chop of helicopter blades could be heard in the distance.

"Are you all right?" Tex shouted over the roar of the fire that was now engulfing the clinic. He moved her to a patch of clear air so that he could inspect her for signs of damage.

"I'm fine," she sobbed and clutched his shirt. "But I don't know where my pig is!" Squinting into the shadows, she again called for him, but Toto did not come.

"Come, pig!" she demanded, her heart lurching into her throat. "Toto!" Her voice broke. She half screamed half sobbed, her head turning this way and that, her gaze darting about. "*Totoooo!*" It was not like Toto to disobey. At least not anymore. He wouldn't have gone back inside. Would he? Tex had told her stories about heroic pigs. Had he gone back in to make sure all the dogs were out?

"Tex, why isn't he coming to me?" Tears, not simply caused by the smoke, began to well in her eyes. "I have to go back in there!"

The woof of the chopper blades drew nearer.

"No way!"

"But, Tex, I have to!"

"Absolutely not! You can't go back in there, Charlotte!" Releasing her wrists, he cupped her cheeks in his palms. "Sweetheart, no amount of inheritance is worth getting yourself killed over."

"But," she sobbed, consumed with fear and grief, "Toto saved my life!"

Before he could react, she twisted away from Tex's grasp, and dashed back into his office, heedless of the warning shouts from behind.

Never in his entire go-round on this planet had Tex been so terrified than when Charlotte disappeared back into the roaring inferno that had become his office. And, in those endless moments of insanity as he searched for her, and finally found her, he knew with unmitigated certainty that he could never live another moment without Charlotte Beauchamp at his side.

And now, as he looked down at her porcelain complexion as she lay in her hospital bed, he knew he loved her without reserve. Would give up his animals for her. Would give up his career for her. Would give up his life for her.

"Hey, sleeping beauty." Tex leaned over and lightly kissed Charlotte's cheek as finally she began to stir. Relief flooded his soul. "I was beginning to wonder if you were ever going to wake up."

Ever so slowly, Charlotte opened her eyes and blinked against the bright, fluorescent lights overhead. "Where am I?" she whispered.

"The hospital. It's nearly three in the morning. You were a very lucky girl, Charlotte Beauchamp. We made it out of my office, just before it blew to smithereens."

"Why did you come home from the conference?"

Tex rolled his eyes. "It appears that Wally forgot to load my briefcase with the correct files. My speech burned up with everything else."

She groaned. "He is so, so fired." Her eyes suddenly flew open and she gripped his hand. "Toto?"

"He's fine. So are all of the dogs. Thanks to you." He leaned forward and kissed her cheek, then chuckled. "Your meal ticket is just as fat and sassy as ever. I tried to bring him with me, but they don't allow pigs during visiting hours, for some reason."

"He's...not my..." She tried to speak, but fell into a fit of wheezy coughing. Tex held up a cup of water with a straw and Charlotte drank deeply. "Thanks," she whispered. "Toto...he's not my meal ticket."

Their fingers still tightly entwined, Tex leaned forward on her bed, to better hear her smoke roughened voice. "How do you mean, honey?"

"After I talked to you last night, I watched that video I told you about. The one from Nanna's safe."

Tex nodded.

"There were some papers with it. A will. A new will."

He frowned. "Really?"

"Mmm-hmm. Nanna must have paid someone to come videotape her when I was out shopping or something, because I had no idea what she'd done. Anyway, when she wasn't laughing herself silly, she said that the first will had been a joke and that I inherit everything—which from what I understand is a sizable chunk of money—as soon as I see the videotape and then contact her lawyer." Charlotte rolled her head on the pillow and smiled. "Nanna Dorothy always did have a nutty sense of humor. Anyway, from what I gather, she thought my having to take care of Toto would force me out of my shell."

Tex stared at her, then started to laugh. "You risked your life for that pig, and he isn't worth a red cent?"

"To me, he's priceless," Charlotte argued. "He saved my life."

"Oh, Charlotte Beauchamp, I love you." Tex laughed till Charlotte feared he might burst a blood vessel.

"Tex," she sighed, "You are more like Nanna Dorothy than is complimentary."

He sighed and wiped his eyes. "I wish I'd known her."

"Me, too." Nostalgia warred with happiness beneath Charlotte's breast. "And Tex?"

"Hmm?"

"I love you, too."

Without waiting for an invitation, Tex climbed into bed beside Charlotte and cradled her in his arms. "If I asked you to marry me, you wouldn't be doing it for the money, would you?" he teased.

"I won't if you won't."

"I promise. So. You're rich. That's hilarious."

"Yes, but even so, I still want to keep busy. I want to fund research for blindness. And guide dog projects." She shrugged. "And I still want to find a job. Something to get me out of the house. Something that will hold my interest until we—" she blushed "—settle down and start a family."

Reaching up, Tex smoothed her hair over the pillow and kissed her on the tip of the nose. "Well, you'd be in luck. I just had to fire this guy that worked with me, and I'm going to need an assistant to help me organize a newer and bigger animal behavior clinic. One that I'm going to build on my own spread. Want to apply for the job?"

"What's the pay?" Charlotte asked saucily.

"A lifetime of hugs and kisses. And maybe some kids and dogs and goats."

"And a pig?"

"And a pig."

"Baby, you've got yourself a deal."

Smiling, Tex brought his lips to hers for a kiss that had Charlotte soaring with a freedom she'd never known before.

Epilogue

"Ah-hem!" Big Daddy tapped the microphone and then blew noisily across the windsock. "This thing on?" he yelled.

"Yes!" Laughter rippled through the crowd that had gathered on the crisp, October day to celebrate at Tex and Charlotte's wedding reception. Tex and Charlotte looked up from where they sat nuzzling one another at the head table and grinned at their uncle.

"Good!" Big Daddy chortled. "In that case, I'd like to make a toast." He held up his glass. "Here's to the beautiful Beauchamp women, and their excellent taste in men. May my nephew, Tex, and his lovely wife, Charlotte, be blessed with the happiness that I have found with Miss Clarise Beauchamp Brubaker."

Miss Clarise blushed prettily and batted the air as she stood slightly behind her husband.

"I'm a lucky man," Big Daddy continued, loving the fact that his audience was captive. "Five of my own kids have already made the trip down the aisle and now three of my brother's boys are enjoying connubial bliss. Not that I'm counting mind ya, but I am still ahead on this deal by two.'' He playfully eyed the table that seated Georgia, Mary, Ginny, Lucy and Carolina. ''Unless y'all have something to announce?''

''No!'' they all shouted in unison, then laughed.

''Well, I'm gonna have to do somethin' about that.'' He turned and gleefully eyeballed his wife. ''We got us some pretty decent lookin' boys round these parts, right, sugarplum?''

''Now, Big Daddy, you leave those poor girls alone.''

''But, honeylips, it's time for Charlotte to throw the bouquet.''

''Big Daddy.'' Miss Clarise's voice held friendly warning.

Laughing, Charlotte stood and gathered her voluminous satin skirts. ''It's okay, Miss Clarise. I have to admit, I'm a bit curious to see who might be next myself.''

Holding her husband's hand, Charlotte moved from the head table to the center of the brick area they'd been using as a dance floor. Toto, looking dapper in a bow tie and four homemade spats trotted to the floor after the bride.

A drumroll sounded from the orchestra pit.

Charlotte grinned up at Tex as he gave her a few last minute instructions on how best to lob her bouquet.

''Keep your head up and your elbows locked. Aim high and give it all you've got.'' Tex gestured to a large group of single women, many of whom were his sisters. ''Try to hit one of them.''

''Gotcha. Okay. Here goes,'' Charlotte shouted.

The girls all jumped and laughed and squealed as Charlotte let go of the flowers. Time suspended as the beribboned bunch rotated through the air.

At first, the flowers seemed to be headed toward the women, but then, corkscrewing wildly at the last moment, they curled around and headed over to where a group of grinning cowboys stood looking on with amusement.

The bouquet bounced off Colt's head and landed in his arms. His mouth fell open and the crowd roared with laughter.

"Colt, my boy, looks like yer doomed," Big Daddy roared. "I only hope you can find a little gal 'at makes you as happy as mine makes me."

His face now a brilliant shade of crimson, Colt tossed the bouquet to Hunt who in turn fired it at the group of girls and sent them scrambling. The orchestra struck up a rousing number and again the throng began to dance.

No one—with the exception of a well-dressed pig, a golden retriever puppy and a bleating kid—even seemed to notice when the groom tugged the bride into the rose garden and finished the kiss he'd begun at the altar.

* * * * *

Watch for Carolyn Zane's contribution to

THE COLTONS: BRIDES OF PRIVILEGE,

*a special collection, available this May,
wherever Silhouette Books are sold.*

#1 *New York Times* bestselling author

NORA ROBERTS

brings you more of the loyal and loving,
tempestuous and tantalizing Stanislaski family.

Coming in February 2001

The Stanislaski Sisters

Natasha and Rachel

Though raised in the Old World traditions of their
family, fiery Natasha Stanislaski and cool, classy
Rachel Stanislaski are ready for a *new* world of love....

*And also available in February 2001 from
Silhouette Special Edition, the newest book in the
heartwarming Stanislaski saga*

CONSIDERING KATE

Natasha and Spencer Kimball's daughter Kate turns her
back on old dreams and returns to her hometown, where
she finds the *man* of her dreams.

Available at your favorite retail outlet.

Silhouette®

Where love comes alive™

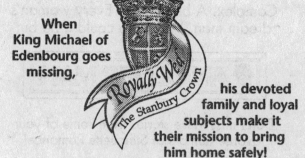

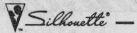

Silhouette®

where love comes alive—online...

your romantic life

Romance 101
♥ Guides to romance, dating and flirting.

Dr. Romance
♥ Get romance advice and tips from our expert, Dr. Romance.

Recipes for Romance
♥ How to plan romantic meals for you and your sweetie.

Daily Love Dose
♥ Tips on how to keep the romance alive every day.

Tales from the Heart
♥ Discuss romantic dilemmas with other members in our Tales from the Heart message board.

SINTL1

Silhouette invites you to come back to Whitehorn, Montana...

MONTANA MAVERICKS

WED IN WHITEHORN—
12 BRAND-NEW stories that capture living and loving beneath the Big Sky where legends live on and love lasts forever!

MM

And the adventure continues...

February 2001—
Jennifer Mikels *Rich, Rugged...Ruthless* (#9)

March 2001—
Cheryl St.John *The Magnificent Seven* (#10)

April 2001—
Laurie Paige *Outlaw Marriage* (#11)

May 2001—
Linda Turner *Nighthawk's Child* (#12)

Available at your favorite retail outlet.

Silhouette®
Where love comes alive™